HEART FOR A HEART

HEART CHRONICLES
BOOK ONE

SEDONA JESSIE

Book Cover by Seventhstar Art
Illustrations by Bibliobean Books
First edition 2025

Paperback ISBN: 979-8-218-64338-6
EBook ISBN: 979-8-218-64337-9

AUTHOR'S NOTE

Please read! HEART FOR A HEART is purely fictional and contains violent scenes, depictions of gore, swearing, and a character being pulled by their hair up a staircase. Some creatures (demons) and scenes may be disturbing.

If you feel that any of which will cause harm to your mental health when reading—please do not read any further.

–Sedona

Playlist

Lucille Ceres

"Libra"–Free Refills
"Peel"–Weakened Friends
"HAMMS IN A GLASS"–Winona Fighter
"Who Is She?"–I Monster

Sebastien Hellebore

"Anchor"–Novo Amor
"In The Woods Somewhere"–Hozier
"i am not who i was"–Chance
"Don't Hate Me"–Badflower
"idontwannabeyouanymore"–Billie Eilish

Seymour Sein

"Oblivion"–Neptunica, Besomorph, Hedara
"Alibi (with Pabllo Vittar & Yseult)"–Sevadaliza, PablloVittar, Yseult
"I Love It (feat. Charli XCX)"–Icona Pop, Charli XCX

Cyx Andromedi

"Picture You"–Chappell Roan
"All I want"–Kodaline
"Your Clothes"–Can't Swim
"Francesca"–Hozier
"Light My Love"–Greta Van Fleet

Good luck.

CHAPTER 1
SEBASTIEN

There was one thing I knew for certain.
I did not murder my father.

I always thought curses were futile—until one was placed upon me. Now, I was stripped of my magic and forced to take the form of a human. Every day was a sharp reminder of my newfound fragile mortality, the weight of the false accusation atop my shoulders, dragging me down like heavy chains.

It had been nearly a century. One grueling, mind-numbing century.

36,183 days, to be exact, but who was counting?

I slid my legs under my desk, the bones of the old wooden chair groaning beneath the shifting weight. For over an hour, I'd been trying to read the complex spells and ancient rituals the elders of the past had used to rally aura molecules from the land—many of which I shamelessly attempted only to be reminded my magic was truly gone. Having found no success other than humiliation, it had been nothing more than a pitiful use of my time. I sighed, running my fingers through my hair, the snarls within the strands catching with a pop.

I rolled my eyes toward a weathered stack of books that towered over me. Being damned to an eternity here had initially sounded dreadful—soul fracturing, really. As the decades passed, with no one else to talk to and no other means of entertainment, these books became my constant companion. Though, if I lost my mind, it would be because I had sequestered myself to another stack.

I spent my first forty years here in a feverish spree of luring and capturing humans to this estate, carving out their hearts just to see if it would lift the curse. To my dismay, it took ninety years before I realized a *willing* human was the key part in my sentencing.

Mother's words echoed in my mind, mocking me.

"The objective for return is to obtain the heart of a willing human."

These past few years, I found myself succumbing to episodes of something akin to dissociation. On occasion, my mind would fracture and wander back to Nyria and the many marvelous territories it held, but it made my soul cry. I would give anything to feel the warmth of Nyria's three suns again. The Human Realm was beyond bleak; nothing more than a trash heap overflowing with vanity and hate. The soilborn had a phrase for this. *The bottom of the barrel.*

The beings here were gluttonous, disastrous rats. It was a wonder the Ethereal hadn't yet eradicated this realm. If I had even a morsel of their prestige, I would have long since drowned this place in fire, even if it meant I would have gone down with it. It would have been a blessing to the realms.

There were times I swore I could feel the humming magic beneath my skin, haunting me like a phantom limb, but I knew it was all in my head. Every futile attempt at casting only fueled my distaste for my situation. Sometimes, it felt like the true purpose of this punishment was to drive me to insanity: I feared it would succeed.

I was doomed to thrive within the confines of this estate—glamored to look like a decrepit infestation of rotten wood that housed rats—though I *could* leave my confines whenever I wish, I felt like a caged animal, nonetheless.

A brash meow pulled me from my self-pitying downward spiral.

I supposed I was not entirely alone.

I blinked, my eyelids rigid, and attempted to force my thoughts back into my mind as a milk-white cat leaped onto the desk, cutting off my view of the book tower. I made a feeble attempt to swat the cat away, resulting in a stack of disheveled books crashing to the floor.

Great.

"Go!" I hissed. The cat peered at me over its shoulder as it padded away, letting out a small growl in response. Irritation writhed within me, as if there were maggots breeding beneath my skin, wriggling throughout my veins. This was the most exciting part of my day.

I glanced past the feline, who had lazily taken position at the base of a gargantuan bookcase, then toward a grandfather clock at the far wall that ticked relentlessly, and sighed. It was 3:53 p.m.

Though time had stopped mattering to me decades ago, I woefully adopted the habit of keeping track. Look at the clock, scour pages, look at the clock, scour pages, and repeat.

Repeat. Repeat.

I pushed myself out of the old chair, ignoring the groaning of its structure, threatening to break.

"I'll have to check the alley ways for a new chair," I murmured as a low grumble emitted from my stomach. I shoved the chair beneath the desk and reached into the pocket of my hole-ridden pants, grabbing onto the black leather lanyard coiled inside. I dangled it in the air in front of me, the slim skeleton key attached to the end seemed to mock me as light reflected off the head where the letter "H" was etched. Why did my mother even bother giving me a key?

I glared at the small piece of metal until my knuckles turned white and my nails bit into the flesh of my palm from clutching it so tightly. Of the decades wasted here, not once had I had the fortune of an intruder.

As I shoved the key back into my pocket, my stomach growled once more.

It never ended!

The most bitter part of being exiled to this realm and bound to this flesh prison of a body, was the necessity of consuming food. Being a nearly immortal being in the Magic Realm had its perks; we required nothing as mundane as physical sustenance for survival, except for occasional sleep.

Here?

The body turned frail and sickly.

I raised my fist to my sternum and raked my knuckles against the wave of bones over my heart, hoping the bruising feeling of bone on bone would gift me a small distraction from, well, everything. Finally, I decided to journey into town, despite knowing it would be nothing short of dreadful. The semblance of freedom was indeed a pleasant surprise when I had first arrived in this realm, but it wasn't nearly enough. The freedom to wander outside of the estate paled in comparison to the freedom of using magic. The freedom of being within my own realm—a name clear of faulty accusation.

"Don't burn the estate down while I'm gone," I grumbled as I made my way across the foyer, knowing only the annoying cat, Seymour, was around to hear—or care. Seymour gave me silence in return, as expected, without bothering to so much as raise his head.

My boots clicked against the floor as I passed endless rows of bookcases. I ran a finger across the spines, scattering dust into the air that shimmered under the candescent light. Reaching the foyer, I grabbed my duster off the round table at its center and tossed it over my shoulders. The coat hung uncomfortably over my frame—the fabric far too loose over me—but it was better than nothing for this inconvenient body. I brushed my hands down the wrinkled front and threw my eyes around the foyer, suddenly feeling like I was being watched.

The walls were coated in black and gold filigree wallpaper with paintings of strangers flowing across them in lines; I was convinced each set of eyes was strategically placed for my mother to watch me struggle and relish in my failure, because I swore, I could feel the eyes watching me. I scoffed.

It would be a waste of aura.

I looked down to the table at my side, its stone legs carved into one large gargoyle, kneeling with palms turned upward to hold the glass top. My eyes met the gargoyles. I had an inkling as to which unfortunate soul Mother had trapped in the vessel, forced to serve eternity here, with me, while holding up a table. Gargoyles *had* always been her favorite way to keep prisoners. Why fill cells, when you could display them in a courtyard or around an estate like little trophies?

Begrudgingly, I stepped toward the table, circling it as I ran my free hand across the top, removing the dust to expose the pressed hellebore flowers that lay beneath the glass. The flowers were a thoughtful touch.

I tugged at the lanyard jutting out of the top of my pocket, pulled the key out, tossed it onto the table over the flowers, and walked out the door.

CHAPTER 2
LUCILLE

I just wanted to reach the next spot of shelter from the angry, raining sky. Taking a long sip of coffee, I noted the subtle hints of nutmeg and hazelnut scorching my tongue, as I pulled out my phone. I needed to find somewhere to loiter while this horrid weather passed.

For a moment, I contemplated heading back to the coffee shop, but it was too packed for my liking. No part of me wanted to sit near others who also decided they needed to get out of the rain, gossiping and gloating over nonsensical things. I'd rather stand out in this shit storm than suffocate in that small building.

It was too easy to stay cooped up when the weather was always gloomy. Every day seemed to be nothing but brooding, weepy clouds. Not seeing the sun for so long, it was enough to drive a girl mad.

I should have just stayed home.

I hadn't been in this town for long, and though I was ready for excitement, choosing today was a poor choice. This weather was beyond disgusting, then there was the brain fog.

Thick clouds clung to my brain, leaving my thoughts murky. I wasn't one to reach out for help, because I was more of a *grin and bear it* and *save the issue for future me* kind of gal. But my recently hazy memory did light a small candle of alarm within me, especially when faint memories occasionally surfaced, featuring a tall, angry man and cheery, petite woman.

Not to mention the incessant pounding behind my temples.

I opened the maps app on my phone, watching the blue line blink, waiting for me to type in a destination.

Where could I hang out while this passed? Another coffee shop? A store?

I looked up from my phone and watched as people raced past me, frantically trying to find their own haven from this downpour. Finally, I used my thumb to type in "library." That seemed like a solid choice because even if it were packed, people *had* to be quiet.

Plus, there was nothing more comforting than hunkering down next to a trove of books. Hitting enter, an address and name popped up and…oh, thank God, it was only a three-minute walk. *That,* I could manage.

"You have arrived at your destination!" chimed the feminine robotic voice from my phone.

I glanced at the map in my hands, then at the library, and back at my phone once more. This place looked more like a mansion than a library. This *was* a weird town in the middle of nowhere, so I supposed this place wasn't *that* bizarre; maybe it was some weird tourist attraction built in hopes of bringing new faces through the town. Regardless, shelter was shelter at this point.

In front of me stood a grand colonial styled edifice heavily engulfed in wet, green vines that crawled their way along the structure. A broad staircase commanded the front, a handful of steep steps leading up to a door so black it was almost as if it had been freshly painted. The brass handle gleamed like a beacon through the dull rainy air, begging to be touched.

I took a tentative step forward but jumped when someone shouted behind me through the sound of sloshing steps. "Careful over there, girl!"

The voice sounded tattered and worn with age. I turned, shielding the relentless rain from my eyes to see an old man jogging through the rain with a newspaper held over his head.

"Nothing but rats, rust, and disease there," he called out over his shoulder as he passed me. "Just sayin'!"

I watched the man continue down the street, his feet slopping through murky puddles that drowned the hem of his pants. Squinting through the raindrops, I turned back to the mansion.

There was some script above the door, but it was nearly impossible to make out what it said other than the word "Library" at the end.

I looked at my phone in my hand, its screen now wet with rain. The pin showed that I was right at my location, so this had to be the library—despite its appearance. Either way, I needed to get out of this weather.

What was it that old guy was hollering about? Haunted rats and rust?

I turned back to the library. The more I *really* looked at it, the older it looked—but not rusty. And I surely hadn't noticed any rodents scampering around here, either.

Maybe that old guy was just old and saying words to just say words. To hell with it.

I sped toward the entrance and barreled up the stairs, avoiding the ivy-strangled railing and ignoring the gray colored water my shoes kicked onto my calves. I reached the door and paused. Apprehension curdled in my gut.

There was a strange yearning in my bones to rush in, but anxious nonsense flooded my mind as my brain battled against other emotions. My subconscious seemingly prodded at my conscious mind, insisting I flee even as my muscles twitched to barge into the waiting warmth.

I looked around while I struggled with indecision. My eyes traced the intricate, dark stained designs of the door; they looked like some sort of flower...pansies, maybe?

Thunder cracked overhead in a deafening roar that made my heart leap into my throat. The malevolent sound shook the windows of the building, the glass panes crackling with what I could only describe as rattled laughter. The sky opened its mouth even wider to vomit buckets of water from its atmospheric intestines.

Here goes nothin'.

CHAPTER 3
LUCILLE

The brass knob of the door was cool against my palm, though the cold of the metal dissipated with my warm touch. With a twist, I put my weight behind the turn. The door opened in a swift motion. Immediately, I was greeted with warmth and a soft orange light.

Warm was good—warm was a step up from the rain. I severed the damp outside world closing the door behind me and looked around the foyer, shaking the length of my coat from my soggy body.

The walls were colored like the night sky had come down to share her darkness with them, broken by faces captured in vibrant oils cast behind glass. A thick film of dust clung to the panes as if they hadn't been touched since they were put up—and all of those eyes seemed to stare right at me. Scant golden filigree lines danced toward the ceiling, looking ghostly as they faded into loose tendrils when they met the ceiling's edge.

My skin crawled, as a shiver slid down my body. I walked toward the center of the room to an ornate round table, the eyes seemed to follow my every move. I forced my feet to continue moving, speeding through the foyer and passing the table, where I noticed a lanyard with a singular key resting.

At least that meant I wasn't alone here.

In my peripheral vision, I could have sworn one of the faces on the wall grinned at me. Another shudder worked its way across my shoulders. I quickened my pace to a jog past the table to an archway that consumed the majority of the opposing wall, like a gaping mouth—yet somehow also like a beacon of safety.

The white marbling of the archway contrasted the dark, dusty room of moving eyes, with soft white marble trim. A looming sense of unease permeated my stomach, clawing through my veins. Maybe it was my imagination, but I swore I could still feel several sets of eyes boring holes in the back of my skull. The urge to turn and flee was strong, but there was also a strange pull, prompting me to keep going.

Stealing a quick glance at my phone, I checked my location again, as if that would somehow dissolve the onslaught of nerves. I tapped my thumb on the pin still highlighted above my location, indicating I was in the library, before stuffing it into my back pocket.

I swear the eyes of the paintings snapped forward when I glanced behind me, toward the door. I would be finding a different exit for when I left, because there was no chance in hell that I would be walking through *that* again.

I ran my fingers over the silken chilled white stone before I stepped through the mouth of the gaping archway. The moment I crossed the threshold, I was greeted with the dense, stagnant smell of aged leather and old paper. The unease in my bones relented at the scent, confirming that I was, in fact, in a library.

Bookshelves stretched up so high in front of me that for a moment, I was convinced the ceiling had to be a mirror. Despite the rows of marble shelves, the floor was inexplicably dark. It looked as if this room was erected from abysmal dark waters—a bizarre and enchanting sight—one I would gladly take over whatever the hell was behind me.

I had never seen a floor this dark; it caused the less logical part of my brain to pull back with the irrational sense that I might plummet into its unknown depths. It was such a contrasting space.

Against my approval, my muscles flexed bringing me to my knees, like the floor begged for my attention. My fingers swiped along the surface of the floor, as if being lulled in by a hypnotic siren song. I almost expected my hand to fall into nothingness, but instead the darkness writhed around from the heat of my fingers touch. I couldn't tell if I was terrified, mesmerized, or both.

Either way, I was beyond curious. Standing and taking a step onto the floor, I couldn't help but watch my feet as I walked toward one of the shelves. The imprint of my footsteps remained on the floor's surface before slowly fading back to black.

My steps echoed brashly against the dark, polished floors. Curiosity writhed like a snake, trying to frantically shed its skin as I found myself in front of a looming bookshelf. A glow emitted from an unknown source, casting a warm golden hue. I slid my finger across the unfamiliar titles as I walked along the stretch of books. I didn't recognize a single one, yet I felt the dull pang of familiarity as my eyes traced over every spine.

I reached for a green book with a lace cover and flipped it open. The first page displayed three overlapping circles with handwritten script scrawled inside each disk. I ran my fingers over the trio, feeling the soft, textured page beneath my skin. Thumbing through the pages, the only things I could understand were the small annotations. Messy arrows pointed to circled foreign words throughout various pages, as if whoever last sifted through this book had been in a frenzied study.

I placed the book back in its spot and snagged another. This one had a black leather cover. The same script was embossed on the front page, the same trio of overlapping circles. I flipped through the pages, once again only able to recognize the three circles alongside more annotations. There was a nagging in my head that clawed at my frontal cortex; the text was like seeing a vaguely familiar face on the street. I thought I recognized something, but muddied memories failed to form a connection.

Whatever.

It made no sense to continue scouring through books when I didn't even understand what I was looking at, but something about this labyrinth of bookshelves drew me in. I weaved through the marble maze, letting my fingers brush over several more spines, freeing them of dust while I stared up at the cathedral-like ceiling yawning above me.

I knew looks could be deceiving in more ways than one, but it made no sense for the ceilings to be so high in this room when its exterior only looked to be two stories. It was as if I were looking up into the sky—it just looked…infinite.

My foot connected with something soft, and I went rigid. *Please don't be a rat, please don't be a rat!*

A cry emitted from the mystery obstacle. I looked down, expecting to find a fat rat scampering away, but was pleasantly met with a petite white cat giving me the dirtiest look as it licked its collision-tousled side.

A pang of guilt hit me immediately.

"Sorry!" I whispered as I crouched, extending a finger as an offer of peace. The cat stared at my finger, then my eyes, then the finger again.

"It was an accident, I swear." I offered the cat my entire hand as it tentatively inched its way closer and closer until its cold nose poked the tip of one of my fingers. The cat pressed its forehead into my palm, purrs erupting from its chest. Its purring, along with those cute little chirps cats sometimes did when they were happy, almost made this bizarre library worth the strange experience.

I quietly laughed at the feline's little sounds as I slid my hand along its smooth back. Maybe it wasn't *so* bad here.

"What a weird place you live in, huh?" I said, continuing to pet the little creature as I looked around.

Just beyond the maze of bookshelves was a large staircase tucked away toward the back corner, its red carpet just peeking through. A little prick of pain shot through one of my fingers, and I yelped in surprise as my focus snapped back to the cat as it pulled its mouth from my hand. *Did this little shit just bite me?*

"Really? You little shit," I mumbled as I glared at the little cat whose back was already turned to me as it trotted away. I pressed the sleeve of my coat to the tiny wound. My knees cracked as I stood, blood rushing to my feet and leaving my eyes filled with tiny black spots.

The cat made a strange sound that seemed to come from

deep within its chest. It stared straight at me—I noticed its eyes were blue rimmed with gold—and shifted from paw to paw as if it were impatiently waiting for something.

"What? *You* bit *me*," I said. The cat whined in response. It stretched and walked a few paces toward me, then turned and walked a few paces back to where it had been. It took a seat, letting out another meow as it squinted at me.

I squinted right back at it.

Was I seriously having a conversation with a cat?

"What could you possibly want? Want me to follow you? I'll follow you, but you have a few screws loose in that little walnut-sized brain of yours if you think I'm going to pet you again." Sure, why not. Let's talk with and follow the weird cat in the weird mansion-library. What is it Alice said?

Curiouser and curiouser.

"Alright, c'mon!" I shooed. "Lead the way, little rabbit." The cat stood to lead me all the way to the far corner of the room toward the staircase, its tail pin straight the entire time as it periodically looked over its shoulder as if to check that I was still following.

CHAPTER 4
SEBASTIEN

The sounds of wet wood scraping against pavement followed as I dragged the chair with one hand, a bag of severely rain-waterlogged scones in the other. It was fine, though; the scones were already stale. The rain was almost a perk, considering I found the pastries in the same alleyway as the second-hand chair I was currently dragging. The moisture will surely soften the scones a little.

This venture was a good one. A sturdier "new" chair and a bag of baked goods? All found in the same alley behind the hot drink stall? That was a win. And this time, no soilborns intervened in my scavenging. If, a century ago, someone had told me that one day I would end up in this rubbish heap of a realm, picking through garbage for chairs and old food, I would have laughed right in their face before decimating them with my aura.

I rounded the corner of the street that led to my glorified prison, shoving the last soggy bit of scone in my mouth before tossing the bag and hoisting the chair over my head to shield myself from the rain. Humans occasionally jogged past me, giving me strange looks before their eyes shone with vacancy as they continued on.

Walking up the stairs to the door, something stirred deep in my chest. Something felt off. Blessedly, the tiniest bit of aura bubbled through the curse and sent out a small, faint alarm through me, telling me someone was in the estate. The sudden sensation of magic nearly knocked me on my ass from shock. I had almost forgotten what my aura felt like. I reached for it again even as it slipped through my mind, frustratingly gone again.

What the hell? How?

I glance toward the estate. Who could have come here? Surely, no human could see this place. That was one of Mother's greatest tricks when she cast me here.

Another Faery? A demon? An assassin from Mother? A giant rat Seymour dragged in? Possibilities flooded my head as I threw the chair over my shoulder like a damsel in distress. I clutched the doorknob, gently pushing it, encouraging the hinges to open in silence as I forced away the wonder of why—and how—a fraction of my magic had broken through the curse. Excitement began to form within me. What does this mean? Is it possible that Mother has forgiven me? I search for the spec of aura that had flitted through my veins just moments ago, still nothing, but that small taste of it had let me know something was off.

I cast my eyes around the foyer as I set the chair down beside the door. Nothing seemed out of place here, though no one from Nyria would ransack this place. If anyone had been sent to kill me, they'd be far more delicate with their entry. I closed the door behind me before heading toward the archway that led to the trove of books.

Taking my lanyard from the table, I positioned the key between my knuckles. It was a pitiful weapon, but I'd killed with less. I peeked my head past the white frame, my hand resting on the cool stone. I kneeled, almost pressing my cheek to the floor as I examined the crescent space in front of me, spotted by small footprints waltzing with Seymour's paw prints.

The floor was made from erydian, the darkest stone in Nyria, mined only from the Hellebore caverns. It was often called the "trail stone" for its ability to keep a reserve of aura. Many manors used this stone because, in the right lighting and from the right angle, it showed the day's footsteps before resetting every morning. It was a great way to monitor areas to see who and what was coming in and out if the space was unattended.

Many families employed trained sentries solely for the purpose of monitoring and studying footsteps and keeping keen eyes on the floors. Though it was an important role, it was often seen as a lowly task in the grand scheme of things. As a youngling, I had loved joining in on training days for the floor sentries. At the time, I had been fascinated by erydian stone tracking, even though others had scoffed and called it a childish, lowly fixation.

I scoffed. It looked like whoever or whatever was here had followed Seymour. If he were smart, he'd lead them to my room until I got home to handle things—but the cat had a brain the size of a walnut, so he probably pranced around, panic-playing cute in hopes that he wouldn't be instantly killed.

At least I didn't smell blood or see any signs of a fight.

I silently followed the footsteps through the bookshelves to where the trail continued up the stairs to the second floor. I heard the faint cadence of a feminine voice trailing from above, my ears tuning into the sounds of the piano that laced through. I placed my hand on the alabaster railing, letting it glide behind me as I stalked toward the voice. A tiny ping of aura wiggled its way through the cracks of the curse again, telling me the intruder was exactly seven paces to the left at the top of the stairs. I grinned, savoring the electrifying feeling hum back to life in my veins, willing it to remain.

"Hello?" I called out in a low sing-song voice. The feminine voice immediately cut off, leaving nothing but the sound of music in its wake. Adrenaline poured through me. It had been so long since I had been in a fight of any kind. This was going to be fun.

"I wasn't expecting a guest today," I purred as I reached the last step. Lunging deeply to my left, I grabbed the body with iron hands.

The intruder let out an ear-piercing shriek as she dug her fingernails into my arm, which I had wrapped firmly around her small frame. My key was in my other hand, pressed against her jugular even as the muscles in my arms protested a little. I couldn't remember the last time I had restrained someone, and this mortal body did not agree with these harsh movements.

The small being thrashed in my grip. I pressed the key further into that precious vein; its blunt edge would be a painfully slow way to die if I were to slice her neck...There was a chance it would take me a few tries.

"Let me go!" squeaked the feminine voice. My skin stung wildly as her nails dug deeper into my flesh, like she was desperate to pluck the tendons from my arm.

"I said let me go!" She thrashed with each word.

From the corner of my eye, I noticed Seymour sprinting

down the hall to our far right.

Coward.

Suddenly, a brutal pain shot up my arm. Stunned, I loosened my grip and jolted back a few steps, my back hitting the wall. Dropping the key, I clutched my arm. My eyes darted to the source of pain. She bit me! The bitch fucking bit me! Blood oozed from the tiny rectangular cuts. Rage filled me. Who the hell would bite? What the hell would bite?

"You filthy little—" My anger turned to bile on my tongue as I looked at the back of the stranger's head. She was a minuscule thing, reaching just below my chest bone. Her hair fell to her elbows in tussled chocolate waves. She immediately turned in my direction, her honeyed eyes frantically flickering from my face to my hands, then to my bloodied arm as fear emanated from her so strongly, I could almost smell the sickly-sweet scent of her terror.

I watched curiously for a breath as she lifted her small hand to her mouth, wiping away dots of my blood from her satiny lips. Something about her—and this scenario—felt familiar. Had I seen her in town? Maybe she reminded me of one of the soilborn I had caught when I first entered this realm.

She spat, the bloodied spit landing a few inches shy of my foot. It bubbled on the surface of the red carpet for a moment before soaking into the fibers. I cringed, my eyebrows shooting up, disgust severing the feeling of *déjà vu*.

Well, if she were an assassin, this would have been more of a fight. If she were a demon, she would have shed that delicate form by now. And if she were a Faery? Well, that would have been obvious as well.

The girl angled her body, like she was readying to dash for the stairs because she thought she got the better of me with the little nip. I'd give her a head start; this was the most exciting time I'd had in this realm since—well, never.

From the corner of my eye, I watched the intruding rat sprint down the stairs. By the sounds of her muffled swears, she'd obviously missed a few steps on the way down. A grin spread on my lips. In such a rush to leave already? Tsk tsk.

I turned to look over the handrail, eyeing the girl as she raced through the maze of bookshelves. I wondered if the jump would blow out these fragile mortal legs. I bent my knees, rocking forward on my toes and judging the distance, weighing the risks and rewards.

"He's trying to kill me," a shrill voice echoed up to me, followed quickly by the sound of fists pounding against a hard surface. "Help!"

How dramatic.

I rolled my neck, vertebrae popping in response. Looking down, I spotted my lanyard and key on the ground. Nudging it with the toe of my boot, I contemplated bringing it downstairs with me. Maybe I could use the strap to—sudden shattering glass interrupted my pondering.

A growl emerged from my throat. Not caring if these knees exploded into a million pieces, I gripped the handrail and hoisted myself over. A loud crack reverberated throughout the estate as my feet planted themselves on the erydian stone below.

A shock wave of color jolted throughout the stone.

Silence followed as her yells ceased, along with the sounds of her destruction of what I assumed was my foyer. I did a quick mental examination of my body, and everything felt fine. I bent my knees just as I did before, forcing my senses to be hyper aware of any pain that might have snuck its way into my bones.

Ha! I was pleasantly surprised that my knees didn't implode, and I could still stand on both feet. It was unexpected, but maybe I'd been underestimating this human husk.

I made my way soundlessly toward the foyer, weaving in and around bookcases as I went. Rounding the corner of a case, I peered around the edge. The air was thick with silence and anticipation. I started to half glide my feet across the slick floor, carefully placing one foot on the small step that led into the foyer I—

"Stay the hell away from me!" she screamed. A splintered picture frame whizzed past me. The fragment barely missed my head as I instinctively avoided the blow by slamming my body to the side of the white mouth of the foyer, my shoulder digging into the marble.

"Let me out of here! Where's the damn door!" the girl hissed. I could tell the little rat was seething, and it made the hair on my arms rise.

I stepped away from the archway, flexing the muscles of my shoulder to push myself away from the column. I plastered a sweet smile on my face. The room was absolutely trashed. I was thoroughly impressed that something so small could do so much damage.

"Stay away from me…Let me out of here," I mocked the

girl smoothly, taking steps closer to her. "Which one is it, rat?" I allowed my eyes to rake slowly over her body.

Her clothes were halfway to being drenched, and that chocolate hair of hers was wild from our earlier struggle. This time, it was unmistakable that the eyes of the pictures were in fact, following me. They no longer made any attempts at concealing their movements.

I knew it. I kept my eyes forward and raised a hand to the paintings, flipping them off, hoping whoever was on the other side would see—hopefully, it was Mother.

My attention was fully on the girl before me, and I took the time to notice her clothes. She wore plain shoes that looked to be formed of rubber and leather, and her trousers were a pale shade of blue in the spots that had dried of rain. Her coat bore similarities to mine. Long, weathered, and neglected. Everything about her appearance was utterly human, but that was impossible.

I had lived in this estate for just over a century, and not once had a human entered of their own volition—only when I had dragged them in—and even then, they were never able to truly see this place. My eyes made their way to the girl's head, where small, frizzy strands protruded at odd angles.

"Hmmm," I hummed as I walked up to the table that encapsulated my family's flowers. I raised my hand slowly to the glass surface and let my fingers drag along the top of its smooth, rounded edge as I continued stalking forward.

My eyes involuntarily picked up the small details of her face. I noticed a spray of beauty marks scattered around her near porcelain skin. It was as if whoever created her had taken their dear, sweet time strategically placing each one. The *déjà vu* from before whispered through my thoughts. This situation was infuriating, puzzling, and exhilarating all at once.

"How did you get in, little rat?" I let the question hang in the air.

"Where. Is. The. *Door*," the girl bit out, each word laced with unmistakable hatred. I dropped my eyes to her small hands that were balled into fists, then met her honey irises.

"I asked you a question first, don't be so rude." I clicked my tongue, stopping just past the table. "*Two* questions, actually."

The girl snapped to her right, lunging and grabbing a shard of glass. I hadn't noticed before, but she had broken nearly every single framed picture in this room. It was as if a tornado had run through it, sparing only the table in its bout of fury. The wallpaper behind the portraits peeled, frayed like wilting flowers. Again, I was impressed by this little thing; she really gave it her all in destroying this space. Her small fist tightened around the shard, red beginning to slick the edges.

"The door!" she barked as she recklessly flung her arm behind her as if to point, her fist making contact with the wall. The shard dropped, shattering as it met the floor, little pieces glistening as the lowlight of the room refracted off the tiny surfaces. Vile words flowed from her lips. The tail end of the fragment must have pushed the glass forward in her grip, slicing her palm. I watched as she bundled up the sleeve of her coat and balled it up in her hand, hissing as she clutched the fabric that turned scarlet with each passing second.

Realization cracked through my skull like a whip, the

feeling snaking through the folds of my brain as things started to piece together. *The door*. With long, frantic strides, I shoved the girl to the side, my hand connected with her tiny, damp shoulder as she squeaked. From the corner of my eye, I saw her flinch at the shove, releasing her wounded hand to catch herself mid fall. The sound of glass grated beneath her feet.

I stared at the perfectly void piece of wall behind her back. It was bare. It was *bare*. Blatantly, utterly, completely bare. Was I losing my mind? I snapped my head from left to right, my hair falling loosely into my eyes. There were lightened spots on the wall where the portraits had been side by side, meeting at the apex of the wall where…the door should have been.

There was no way that I was this negligent of my own surroundings—of my own situation! Of this damn curse! My fingers curled into a fist, my nails cutting crescents into my palms. Manic laughter erupted from me as I threw my head back and howled into the air.

I pivoted in the direction of the girl, feeling something stir within me. She flinched again, probably at the crazed emotions on my face. Unclenching one fist, I jutted my hand out and grabbed a fist full of her hair to give it a harsh yank upwards.

"Get up!" I growled. How could I have been so stupid? Had all these years here dulled my senses that much? Was I really so naïve that I couldn't see what literally walked through my front door? The door that had *vanished* just as this rat had appeared?

The girl stayed limp; her hands layered on top of my own. I could feel her sticky blood seep its way through the balled-up portion of her coat, warming my skin.

31

"Let me go!" she cried. Actual tears streamed down her face, and for whatever reason, this set fire to my veins. Unclenching my other fist, I grabbed another handful of her hair—her *human* hair—and jerked her head sideways as I hauled her toward the archway.

"Seymour!" I bellowed. "Come out, you little snake! It's time!" My feet stomped loudly as I reached the archway with the screaming, crying girl in tow. With a long stride, I took the step down to the erydian floor. I felt the girl's body thud against the surface as her nails dug into the top of my hands.

"SEYMOUR!" I roared, my vocal cords aching with the force. The echo seemed to send a shiver down the estate's nonexistent spine, causing the books that lined the maze of shelves to quiver.

"Stop!" the girl screamed, now openly sobbing. "Please! Please, just let me go!"

Her nails raked and sliced deeper and deeper into my flesh. Her blood from her wound stung against mine as the two mixed.

Sweat beaded along my hairline as we reached the staircase, my hands aching and raw. A feline yowl permeated the air as I hoisted the girl up the three steps by her hair. I glanced over my shoulder, then down at the girl, my lungs aching for air. Was this form so frail that I couldn't even drag a body up some stairs?

It was baffling that I could still function, considering how negligent I had been to this body. Despite my earlier surprise at its capabilities. I could feel my aura stir like a beast slowly waking from hibernation. I stopped at the fifth stair up from the bottom, my fingers still screaming. I examined my hands, which were now bloodied and swollen with long gashes. The girl still clawed at the battered flesh.

"Listen, human. I can either keep dragging you, or you can walk." I tightened my fists on her locks of hair and jerked her forward by her scalp, momentarily giving the top side of my hand a moment of reprieve.

"And walk where? To some room for you to butcher me in?" The girl glared up at me upside down as her lips pursed before a wad of spit catapulted from her satin mouth, landing on my cheek. A growl escaped my throat. I left one hand tangled in her snarled hair and used my free hand to swipe the spit off my face.

"Dragged it is." Utilizing my remaining rush of adrenaline, I took the stairs two at a time. I could feel the girl's body bounce and falter on each step as she rotated under my grip while she attempted to find her footing. Occasionally, I gave her a firm yank when she snagged on a step, but it was really more for my own satisfaction.

I did it.

I passed Seymour at the halfway point on the stairs, his large eyes flickering to the girl, then onto me.

"Useless," I muttered as I passed him without bothering to make eye contact.

My knuckles throbbed as I reached the top of the stairs, Seymour following closely behind. I straightened my spine, arching with relief as my back popped. As I stretched, I looked down at the girl in my grasp. Her face was swollen and salted with dried tears, but she stayed silent.

Finally.

She didn't even whimper as her body lifted off the floor with my stretch. I couldn't continue dragging her. She wasn't heavy by any means, but every second counted, and I'd already wasted too much time chasing her around. Though, I did enjoy the game of cat and mouse—or rather, cat and *rat*. I chuckled to myself, utter delight spreading throughout me.

Seymour padded his way down the hall he had fled to earlier. I let out a sigh. I'd have to reprimand him later. First, I needed to bind her hands. My eyes hovered over everything that lined this narrow mezzanine before stopping at a dark, stained Victorian style chair between two towering bookcases that stretched up to the floor above. Maybe I could tear open the tufted green seat and use the springs as makeshift bonds? No, that would take too much time, and despite this body surpassing my expectations today, I did not think I could unbend and reshape a spring efficiently enough to make worthwhile shackles.

My eyes passed the record player that was nestled next to yet another towering bookcase, the somber harmonic sounds of piano now replaced with the grating sound of skipping as the stylus bounced gently off the track.

I had all these years to prepare for this moment, yet I was so *under-prepared* that it was humiliating. A muffled meow and the gentle scuff of metal sliding against carpet tore me from my self-pity. Seymour stopped just to my left, an old leather belt

34

weighing down his tiny cat jowls. He squinted as a vibrating hum emitted from his throat.

"Imagine that, worm. You've finally decided to make use of yourself." I snatched the belt from his mouth, the leather slick with his drool.

CHAPTER 5
LUCILLE

I was going to die. I was sure of it. Every sector of my mind screamed at me. My *body* seemed to scream at me. The searing pain of my scalp had dissipated into a dull, almost numb, ache.

Maybe I was going into shock. All the fight from before had suddenly disappeared. My eyes stung, wanting to release tears again. I could feel how swollen they had become, along with the salt from the earlier tears crusting along my eyelashes. I couldn't even be bothered to care—I just sat here.

"Give me your hands," the man barked. The words didn't make sense to my ears. I could tell he was jostling my head by my hair, shaking me like some tattered ragdoll, but I could hardly feel his tug anymore. All that I could think was that I was going to die here. I was going to die here. I was going to di—

Suddenly, my neck was pulled backward at nearly a ninety-degree angle, and *this* I felt. His two fists knotted in my hair. The man's hot breath coated my forehead, my broken strands of hair blowing into my eyes.

The base of my neck burned from the angle, the muscles that supported my skull cramping around the delicate vertebrae. I met his eyes and noticed that even though he kneeled on one knee, he still towered over me. I never had a chance against him, and I really thought I could take him. *I was so stupid.*

Despite the feeling of defeat, the pain brought about a microscopic part of me—the brave part—that told me that this wasn't over yet, and I couldn't give up. That I could make it out of here if I kept trying. I bared my teeth at him, still tasting his rancid blood on my tongue.

The man looked deceptively frail and incredibly malnourished. Sure, he was tall. But by no means did he look even a fraction of how strong he actually was. His face was gaunt, but his lips were full. Full and smirking through his hollowed cheeks showcasing his high cheek bones in an unflattering way. The dim lighting only added to his haunting, skeletal look.

I guess I hadn't cared enough to get a good look at him earlier, but with those hate-filled eyes that were so green that they mimicked the ivy that covered the exterior of this place, he looked absolutely feral. He was a brooding storm personified.

"I will not ask again," he snarled as he tugged my head further back, further exposing my throat. I could feel the muscles at the base of my neck spasm and cramp as my back arched in an attempt to compensate for the position.

I clenched my jaw and pooled up any bit of saliva I could and spat it straight up onto his chin. I shot my hands up toward his face, aiming for his eyeballs, my fingers curled into claws. I just missed as he jerked back in the same moment as if he had anticipated the strike. A growl escaped me, but I felt a small twinge of satisfaction as I watched my spit run down his chin to his neck.

"Such a vile little creature," he growled, distaste filling

his eyes. "Is that all you're capable of doing? Spitting?"

He loosened the vise-like grip of one of his hands and swiftly grabbed both of my wrists into his singular grasp. Amidst the broken strands of my hair that were littered between his fingers, I noticed the damage I did to the tops of his hands and smirked. At least I had left some marks on him, because my adrenaline was quickly dwindling. Releasing my scalp, he used his freed hand to wipe the spit that was now running down his throat, leaving the back of my head to crack against the floor.

It felt as though talons were clawing their way through the soft folds of my brain. My head pulsed in agony as pain radiated through my eyelids. I winced. I could feel *everything*. My hips and lower back felt tender to the bone.

Muffled voices surrounded me, but the sounds were so muddied it was as if they were talking underwater. My body gently rocked side to side, the movement causing sharp pain to spear through my hips. Suddenly, it dawned on me that I was moving.

Did that twig of a man think he had killed me?

Maybe he was driving me somewhere to dump my body, and based on the subtle movements, that felt like a solid guess. I cracked open an eye. My poor weak eyelid struggled greatly to flutter open, as if each eyelash had been individually held down by anchors. I couldn't see. There was no difference whether my eyes were open or closed, because it was all darkness.

My stomach twisted as I tried to focus my senses through

the searing pain that pulsed through my skull. Surely, I would have been able to tell if I had a blindfold on, or if that walking skeleton of a man had put something over my head. There was no way that I wouldn't be able to at least see—*holy shit*.

My mind flashed through the last few moments that I could remember before I blacked out. I could recall most of the fight, him pulling my neck back, binding my hands, and... and then hearing the crack of my skull hitting the floor.

The knot in my stomach twisted tighter as bile began to slick the back of my tongue. I swallowed it down. *He'd blinded me. That asshole had blinded me!* Had I hit my head that hard? That didn't seem possible, the floor was carpeted.

How long had I been out for? I honestly wasn't sure if that was something I actually wanted to know, but the realization that my vision had been obliterated soured in my gut.

Bile rose in the back of my throat once more, this time there was no chance of evading the inevitable. I attempted to twist my body, but at its protests, I settled for turning my head just as my stomach convulsed. Vomit pooled in the pocket of my cheek as my choked coughs caused it to spill over the corner of my mouth.

Was I seriously about to choke on my own vomit? My stomach seized again as my abdomen pulled tight from the involuntary contractions. I felt the warm, putrid liquid as it ran from my mouth and down my cheek.

Suddenly, a warm hand grabbed my shoulder, and another one slid beneath my hip. My body attempted to tense at the touch, but there was no fight left in me as embarrassment ebbed its way into my mind at the realization that someone had just watched me heave my insides onto my own face. I winced internally, pushing past the fleeting feeling.

What did I have to be embarrassed for? Hell, I hope whoever was touching me had to clean all that up.

The hand on me gingerly tipped me over onto my right side. I attempted to raise my head to hack out a wet, gurgling cough, but the movement had made it feel like an anvil was repeatedly bashing my brain. Despite my best efforts to keep my head raised, it dropped nearly in the same instant, landing right into the puddle of my own puke.

What a way to go out, at least I went out with a half-assed fight.

Muffled voices flooded my ears again, sounding as if people were arguing around me.

I felt someone blow into my ear, almost like a lover would do to coax their partner to wake. But the breath felt hot— *really hot.* And not in a romantic way. It was as if a molten worm had been dropped down my ear canal. The hot air slithered millimeter by millimeter, deeper and deeper. As the hot worm made its way to the deepest internal corner of my ear, sounds became clearer.

Was this what it was like being on death's door? I had always imagined it would have been a sense of euphoria following a mental slide show of my life flashing before my eyes—but this? This felt more like a fever dream, and I desperately wanted to wake up and shake off.

"I said, *watch her.* If she dies, our exile will be *permanent.* Can you seriously not take simple orders? Did all that time spent as a cat warp your brain that much?" A low voice cracked with irritation.

"I *am* watching her. You didn't hear her choking on her own vomit? Seriously." The warm hands left my body, leaving me to rock in my puke puddle. "Can't humans get concussions, or whatever? From hitting their head too hard? Can't they die from that? Or uh, hm. How about *asphyxiation*? You spent so much time dawdling in this realm and you didn't learn the basic things that can kill one of these? Shouldn't *you* be healing her?" This voice was animated with sarcasm.

Someone exhaled loudly as feet stomped toward me. A new set of hands were on me in an instant. I could tell these belonged to someone else, because these were much rougher as they roughly placed one hand on the top of my shoulder while the other pushed at the side of my face. I stifled my breath as I felt my cheek squish into the rancid bile while the hands rifled through my hair.

"She's fine. It's just a gash. She didn't hit her head that hard. The blood has already clotted. It doesn't matter regardless. If she's breathing, she's good." The stranger let go abruptly, letting my head rock back into the puddle.

There was a pause, and somehow, I could tell several sets of eyes were on me. The energy around me seemed to shift, and the stomps receded.

"The condition of her body means nothing as long as her heart still beats. *That's* what matters, got it? Now, get her up. She smells rancid. Do something about that. We might have made it through the portal, and I don't want to be walking with something

41

that smells like spoiled meat."

There was a creak, then the sound of someone sitting.

"Ignore him," someone stated so softly that I had barely heard it. "Can you hear me?"

I felt the soft touch of the stranger from before as their hands gently brushed my hair from my face before pressing something cold against it. A cloth? Gentle swipes of fabric ran along my cheek, then down my hair. The stranger slid one hand underneath my head, while their other hand found my ribcage. My body made a feeble attempt to tense again, their touch left me feeling utterly vulnerable.

Suddenly, I was being moved and propped upright. Whatever I was in—maybe a train—went over a bump, and the movement caused my battered body to sway and almost topple. Someone clicked their tongue and repositioned me again, so that I leaned against something hard.

"This is no way to be," the person whispered, their voice so low that I could barely hear it. "I'm so—"

"Un-cast her eyes. We've almost reached our stopping point. We will be traveling on foot, and I have no intentions on carrying that thing. So, unless one of you two plan to do it, get to it."

A slow sigh followed those words, and warmth bloomed behind my eyelids. That warmth—though brief—was pleasant, and the pain overwhelming my brain subsided for a small breath.

"Come on, soilling, open up those eyes." Merciful hands nudged my shoulder. I didn't *want* to open my eyes again. For what reason? To be reminded that I had been abducted? To see nothing but an empty abyss? Pass. Resolve filled me as I pressed my eyelids shut.

Just kill me already.

"No can do." The voice chuckled.

Had I said that out loud?

Going over another bump, we came to a staggering halt. This one threw me to the side, and I instinctively reached out to catch myself. My wrists stung, and the wound on my palm from before splitting open at the attempt.

The person chuckled as they propped up again. The sound of heavy steps rang out in front of me as someone else made their way to me.

"C'mon filth. Up! Open your eyes already," an angry voice commanded.

I remained still. I knew that my best chance of survival was with compliance, but I'd be lying if I didn't say I wasn't one stubborn bi—

"I said, up!"

Violent hands snatched my bound ones with a harsh yank. My stiff shoulders cracked, and my feet flew out from beneath me. Leather bit painfully into the flesh of my wrists. I attempted to press my feet downward, but my toes skimmed along the floor. I stifled a wince, my joints crying from the abrupt movement.

A rough hand grabbed my face and squeezed my cheeks, causing them to press against grooves of my teeth—the hand felt giant against my skin as a coarse finger freed itself from my cheeks and pried my left eyelid open.

I flinched as harsh, bright light assaulted my eye. For a

moment, I saw nothing but white and a faint mix of colors—relief filled me. I wasn't blind.

If eyelids could crack, that's what mine would have done. My *eyelids* felt stiff. Begrudgingly, I opened my other eye. If I planned on trying to save myself, I needed to try to visually compile everything about my captors, the vehicle, or at the least the landscape. Anything notable that I could relay to someone of authority—or even a stranger—who could help me.

The moment my eyes adjusted to the light; the first unfortunate thing I saw was a familiar set of malice-filled green eyes that were too close for comfort. I jerked my head back and scowled.

The green-eyed man released my face and straightened, leaving me to stare right into his leather clad chest. He let go of my aching wrists, my knees buckling. It took all my strength to avoid crumbling into the pile of my vomit that was just inches away.

His hand suddenly jutted out; a leather pouch choked in his grasp.

"Water. Drink." He shoved the pouch against my chest.

I eyed the suede bag warily, then looked at the green-eyed man's face. There was something achingly familiar about that face, but my fog-filled brain was having a hard time sifting through thoughts to pinpoint where I had seen him before. He looked down at me with nothing less than pure disgust.

"If I wanted you dead, you'd be dead," he said with a smirk so vile it made my heart clench. "It's not poison. Drink, or I will force you to drink." He pressed the pouch harder against my chest.

Hesitantly, I reached for it with my bound hands, but it slipped through my fingers just as I was about to grasp it. I scoffed and glared at him. The corner of his mouth ticked upwards as he huffed a laugh before walking away and leaving me with the pouch at my feet.

"Asshole," I mumbled.

I kneeled to grab the pouch and noticed that the floor was composed of sun-washed wooden planks which groaned under my shifting weight as I pawed at the pouch. The clear liquid had already begun to stain the wood where it had leaked. Successful at last, I clutched it between my hands and lifted the opening to my lips. There were a few mouthfuls of water left, and the moment it hit my tongue, I swear I could feel each cell in my body absorb the liquid.

The floor suddenly dipped as it bobbed with the shifting of weight followed by the sound of feet hitting dirt. I turned toward the sound, watching as three large men hopped out from the open back. It dawned on me that I had been crouched in the back of a rather large carriage. Not a cute, delicate carriage, but an actual near-medieval carriage. My brows pulled together as I finally glanced around the space that I was in.

Aged iron laced the inside like a ribcage with worn wooden benches against the outer walls with thin moody maroon cushions on top. My eyes followed the row of benches to the open back to where three men stood just a few feet away.

Sunlight drenched their bodies as if the sun itself had decided to wrap his arms around each. Of the three men, I took in the green-eyed asshole first. He looked familiar in a way I couldn't understand through my hazy brain. His hair fell over his eyes in lazy black waves that stopped right at his shoulders. With a smooth swoop, he brought a hand up and tossed his hair from his venomous eyes, leaving a raw shock of beauty in his hair's absence. The sun caught a dagger strapped tightly to his biceps— unsettling, but not surprising. It took everything for me to peel my eyes from that face.

I noted that the tops of his hands were marred as if he had stuck them in a box full of feral cats. I squinted, forcing my brain to form a clearer image despite the sun stinging my corneas and the fog in my mind. *Was this the same guy from the library?*

They bore a resemblance to one another, but that guy was much gaunter and more hollowed out. No. This face was full, chiseled, and bore an irritatingly well-formed jawline. His cheeks were not sunken in but contoured naturally. Honestly, his jawline alone had looked annoyingly perfect enough, the rest of it just added insult to injury. My eyes hovered once more on the blade strapped to his arms. He really could have killed me if he had wanted to.

CHAPTER 6
LUCILLE

One of the other men slapped the green-eyed one hard on the shoulder, just above the weapon. Though Green Eye's jaw flexed, and his body tensed with annoyance, his face remained stoic as he clenched and unclenched his fists.

The man beside him was of equally towering height, with hair that fell in long moonlight painted strands past his shoulders. His skin was nearly glowing gold in the sunlight, and the casual white linen-like ensemble he wore contrasted beautifully with his honied skin and cerulean eyes. I allowed my eyes to devour this heathen as well—why not? He was stunning too. A wide bright smile was on full display as he lowered his hand from Green Eyes' shoulder, resting it at his hip. These damned, beautiful bastards.

"Are you going to stand there and gawk?" I hadn't noticed that Green Eyes had been staring at me, watching me stand in the darkness of the back of the carriage like an utter fool as I ogled the sun-blessed one in white as if he were an animal in an enclosure at the zoo.

Heat flooded my cheeks. I opened my mouth, unsure of what to even say.

"C'mon now, Bas! We just stopped moving. The girl's been knocked out for a while. I'm sure that tiny human brain is overwhelmed, just give her a second." The man in white hit me with a golden smile—one of those "come run into my arms" type of smiles—and let out a slow, low whistle while shaking his head. "What I would give to see Nyria with fresh eyes."

Nyria? My eyes flickered to the smiling man beside the one called Bas. He looked at me with such kind eyes. He had to have been the one that was helping me earlier. The carriage shifted beneath my feet as if something had shoved it from the front. My toe caught an uneven board, and I stumbled forward, my bound hands stretched out in front of me, preparing to brace for my fall as a flash of gold and white blurred in my periphery.

"Watch yourself! Careful now, human!" Hands grabbed me around the waist and effortlessly lifted me before I connected with the ground.

How the hell? I stared up at him with wide eyes, unsure how he had gotten to me so quickly.

"Can't have the guest of honor getting too injured, can we?" The kind one beamed down at me as he lowered me. My feet found the ground with ease, his hands secure around my waist. I was suddenly hyper aware of how filthy I was against the contrast of his bright, white clothes, and just gaped at him, my mouth opening and closing like a fish.

"Thanks?" I managed to stammer. The skin at the corner of his eyes crinkled as he nodded, acknowledging my words.

He angled me and pulled me in front of him so I faced the other two men. Then, he lowered himself to be eye level with me, his cheek just inches from mine as he gestured to the others, almost as if he were presenting them to me. "We have a long journey ahead of us, so let's get some introductions out of the way!"

His hair fell over my shoulder as if it were my own, his lavender scent suddenly infiltrating my nostrils. I turned my head slightly, meeting his eyes as he continued.

"I'm Seymour." He winked, then pointed to Green Eyes. "You and Bas already met back at the estate."

Bas's gaze was already burning holes into me when my eyes met his. He looked at me with such unwarranted disgust, as if my presence was the biggest burden of his life—as if I had chosen to be here, to weasel my way into their little group. His glare was heavy, like weights pressing into my sternum. I settled on staring at the space between his eyebrows, hoping my returned look was unwavering, as well.

"That other brute there is Cyx." Seymour loosened a breathy laugh and lowered his hand as he straightened. "And you, soilling? Your name?"

I looked from Bas to Cyx, who stood like a giant among us. His hair had been pulled back into a rough bun at the base of his neck, setting his face on full display. Unfortunately, he looked just as sickeningly perfect as the others. I fought the urge to roll my eyes. It would have helped if they had all been ugly. But nope. The three men who took me were painstakingly gorgeous. I would have to really try to keep my emotions in check.

There was something about Cyx that I couldn't quite put my finger on. It was the way he stared me down, those mossy-brown eyes sliding over my body several times as if cataloging every inch of my being. The way his arms folded over his chest, the material stretching across his shoulders. I couldn't help but steal a glance at his biceps—to scan them for weapons, of course!

49

The leathers that hugged his arms were bare, which granted me a bit of relief, but part of me knew those slots likely wouldn't be empty for long.

Seymour was still talking, but I was fully enamored by Cyx. Questions scratched at the walls of my mind. It was as if the more I looked at him, the more the world tunneled around me. The sheer energy that radiated from him was nothing short of suffocating and intoxicating. My eyes found his again, and I realized he was staring at me with an intense curiosity that probably twinned my own. What was it about him that perplexed me? Why was there such a puzzling sense of familiarity about him?

A hand jostled my shoulder.

"Hello?" Seymour sang, invading my vision with a warm hand as he grinned. "Do you have a name, soilling? Or do we get the pleasure of naming you ourselves?"

Tearing my eyes from Cyx felt as though I was trying to lift a boulder with my bare hands, but Seymour was persistent.

"Lucille," I stated, the word raspy and grating as it left my throat. Seymour's grin grew into something utterly feline.

"Welcome to the Second Realm, Lucille," Seymour beamed, lifting his face to the sky.

CHAPTER 7
LUCILLE

"Second Realm?" I repeated.

He shrugged. "The Human Realm is earth. Magic Realm, Nyria. Ethereal Realm…" He waved a hand around lazily.

"This is a waste of time," growled Bas. He stomped toward me, and I fought the urge to shrink in on myself. His lip curled up in disgust as he pushed past me, throwing me off balance. The scent of his warmed leathers mixed with a hint of clove and cinnamon lingered in the hot air in his wake.

What was his deal? *He* took *me*.

Bas had brushed my coat off my shoulder, exposing my second layer of clothing to the warm breeze. Seymour clicked his tongue as I shifted my shoulder in an attempt to shrug off the remainder of my coat, only to remember my hands were still bound.

With the movement, I noticed the soreness in my bones had subsided at some point. But why was it so hot? I could feel my sweat pool beneath my heavy layers. I settled for letting my coat drape around my back and sag into the dirt as it hung off my elbows.

I turned toward the sound of Bas's steps, my eyes falling to the open-backed carriage that stood paces away. Its roof was nothing more than a delicate gossamer fabric that rippled in the thick air as it hung around the rib cage-like structure. Tiny iridescent sparkles flashed as a hot breeze blew through the fabric and into the husk of the carriage. The bottom cradle of the carriage was a rich maroon, adorned with intricate black flowers embossed into the wooden underbelly. The flowers seemed to dance around one another across its surface, leaves and stems intertwining like partners in a waltz.

I scoffed because it looked more and more absurd the longer I stared at it. When I looked up and back toward the sheer roof, my breath snagged in my throat. I had been so wrapped up with eyeballing these heathens and their gaudy carriage, that I hadn't even bothered to look at my surroundings.

I blinked hard, lifting my bound hands up just above my eyes as they adjusted to the light. The land was awash by the brightness of not one, but *three* suns. Everything was so vibrant. Too vibrant. The suns sat proudly in the sky in a near perfect row, ascending in size. It was a wonder that the sky could remain such a rich cobalt—surely that amount of light should have washed out everything it touched.

White spots danced in my vision, and my eyes began to burn.

"You know, you'll go blind if you stare at the sun for too long, right?" Someone chuckled behind me—*Seymour*. I pressed my eyes closed, pushing the heel of my thumbs into them and waited for the dancing dots to take their leave.

I dropped my hands to find Seymour grinning beside me.

"Where are we?" I asked, my voice stronger than it had been before.

My eyes caught Cyx's, who had been standing in the same spot as before, his eyes still on me. A long dirt road stretched behind him, crowded by a flood of moss-cloaked trees on each side, the sun-soaked dirt a shocking orange.

"As I said, the Second Realm—Nyria." Seymour threw his arms wide. Though his words were slow and careful, he proudly gestured around him, the linen sleeve shaking with his arm. "You know, the Magic Realm."

A bout of laughter bubbled in my throat.

Does this guy think I'm dumb? *Magic Realm.* I brought both hands to my face and pressed the heels of my palms against my sore, sun-bit eyes and rubbed.

"Right. Hilarious, but no, really. Where are we? If one of you drugged me, you can just say so. No need to lie or play with me. I mean, you already kidnapped me." My laughter cut in between my words, I probably sounded hysterical. I was starting to freak out a little—granted, I probably should have been much worse. The suns, the men, that damned carriage. Between being dragged by my scalp, knocked out, and waking up here—wherever *here* was—I should be much more freaked out.

My eyes wandered back to Cyx, whose leather clad arms were still across his chest. This time when our gazes locked, it was as if I could see the weight of the world in his eyes as I tried to convey my desperate need for understanding. But the effort fell flat as he averted his eyes first.

"This is a complete waste of time," Bas said out of nowhere. He sneered as he stalked over to me. "Introductions are pointless. She is nothing more than an accessory from here on out.

A vessel. I don't need you getting attached to this thing."

His eyes locked with Seymour's. The word "thing" leaked from his lips like poison, the toxicity behind that one word made me want to wrap my hands around his irritatingly pretty neck and squeeze until his eyes popped.

"She's nothing more than filth," Bas continued, his eyes meeting mine. A smirk tugged at the corner of his lips as if he could read my mind, his voice saturated with contempt. "A filthy *human*. A soilborn, useless rat. So, shut up. Let's move. We have no time for this nonsense. The nedeer need to be released. We'll leave the carriage behind. We're on foot from here until we reach the Amisa waterway."

"I was just trying to show kindness." Seymour's hands fell to his sides as he took a step in my direction as if to apologize, as if he felt bad for me. The subtle gesture felt like an intrusion—a reminder of my vulnerability. What was this guy's motive?

My mind was in turmoil as I struggled to make sense of their actions. Seymour was being nice, but nice guys didn't typically aid in abductions. Bas, on the other hand, seemed like the leader of this group, and he made it clear he had no issues with bossing people around.

A deafening crack reverberated, and my heart skipped a beat. It took me a moment to realize the sound had come from beside me. My eyes widened in shock as Bas threw Seymour into the dirt, his face was twisted with sickening anger.

"Hey!" I yelled before I could think about why or what I could even do in this situation.

"Listen to me," Bas growled, his voice low and

dangerous. "You insolent worm. You were trying to show kindness? She is not a guest in our lands. She is nothing more than a vessel, *if* that. She does not need kindness. Do you hear me?"

Bas's boot slammed down hard on Seymour's back once, twice, a third time. Seymour's body jolted, and his arms flexed as he planted both palms onto the saffron colored dirt.

Bas towered over Seymour; his jaw set in rage as his eyes narrowed. To my surprise, Seymour didn't so much as cower. No, he remained unwavering in place, as if he expected and welcomed these verbal lashings and strikes—like this happened often.

Bas pressed harder against Seymour's back. The orange from the bottom of his cracked leather boot stained the pristine white linen of Seymour's shirt.

"I asked if you heard me!" Bas bellowed.

"Hey! What are you doing?" I yelled out again, bewildered at what was unfolding before me. *This guy was insane!*

I stepped toward the two men. From the corner of my eye, I saw Cyx step with me in tandem. We both froze.

"Yes—" Seymour bit out, his tone submissive, but not quite meek. He tried to lower his head, his hair falling around his face like a long pale curtain. "My Prince." The words sounded spoiled as they hung in the air, a peculiar essence of resentment laced within them.

"*Prince?*" I stared at Bas, his towering figure looming over Seymour's body beneath his foot. His eyes snapped to mine, and he stiffened, as if he had forgotten I was standing just a couple feet away the entire time.

"*You* do not get the pleasure of calling me Prince, Bas,

nor even Sebastien. *You* are lucky I don't cast that unfortunate, soilborn mouth of yours." He spat at my feet, the saliva just missing my foot.

He was so easy to set off, I couldn't quite resist responding. "So, what am I supposed to call you then?"

"Which part did you not understand? *Nothing*. Take this as a royal order, you do not have permission to even speak to me. You are to simply exist and follow my orders. Does that make sense to you, or is it too complex for your tiny brain? Be grateful you even had the pleasure of hearing my name fall from the lips of another."

My eyes rolled so deep into my skull; I wondered if I'd swallow them.

CHAPTER 8
SEBASTIEN

"Get up!" I barked at Seymour, pressing my heel into the back of his shirt and leaving a smear of vibrant soil until he attempted to rise.

Just as he got up on all fours, I kicked my heel downwards so he slammed face first into the dirt.

I could not have anyone disrespect me in front of something as lowly as a soilborn.

I turned to the frail human beside me, her small figure casting a delicate shadow over Seymour's body. I thoroughly enjoyed the way her face twisted in disgust, and the way her eyebrows pulled together—I could drink it in for a lifetime. Despite those full lips being dry and cracked, her hair matted with filth, and the fact she smelled like she'd been dragged through hell and back, my heart clenched at the sight of her. Through all the grime, her beauty still forced through.

If her eyes had claws, I'd be in ribbons.

"What is wrong with you?" she exclaimed, moving toward Seymour as if she could hoist him from the ground herself.

How would her body hold up in Nyria? I couldn't recall a time when a human had entered our realm, but I assumed it would likely wreak havoc on her system. Though, she's shown no signs of such yet. In fact, she seemed to be getting stronger and stronger each minute.

What a fascinating little thing—Nope, no.

I quickly snuffed any shred of emotion that tried bubbling up from deep within me, swallowing it down into the pits of my being. It made no sense for my heart to react this way, considering she would experience far worse once Mother got her hands on the soilling.

She was just our ticket home. We just had to make it to Hellebore.

I glanced at Cyx, jealousy suddenly rooting itself in my chest as he stood, unmoving. His eyes were also fixed on the human, and the sight made me want to ignite those orbs in his skull and watch them melt. As far as I was concerned, he got the worst of Mother's curse, but that didn't eliminate the layers of jealousy I felt for him then and now—and unfortunately, now in more ways than one.

While Seymour and I were given some semblance of freedom in the Human Realm, Cyx had been confined into the tomb of a gargoyle, trapped in solitary confinement until our key to freedom arrived. It was a strategic move on Mother's part. After all, he was a Portal Mage. He hadn't been stripped of his aura like me and Seymour.

Unlike other magic folk, a Portal Mage's aura was deeply rooted with powerful ties to the Ethereal Realm. Portal Mages could harness some serious raw power. But Mages as a species had always been reasonable and respectful. Though they were scarce, they never expressed the desire to take advantage of anyone or any situation. Irritatingly humble assholes.

For Seymour and me, the curse may have restrained our abilities to wield aura, but for Cyx, it wouldn't have been able to completely suppress his abilities unless he was physically restrained. Turning him into a gargoyle was the best solution for Mother. I assumed he had been sent with us to be nothing more than a means of travel if the chance ever arose that a human would enter the estate. And here we were—and here *he* was, drinking her in, as well.

"Now that we all remember our places and that I'm in charge here, I will release the nedeer, seeing as some of us lack the competence to understand the situation we are in. One of you, grab the human. Restrain her, cast her. I don't care. Whatever you feel is necessary." I turned my eyes to Seymour. "Do not waste any more time."

I left Seymour and Cyx to figure things out between themselves, their voices fading into a distant murmur as they discussed what to do with the human as I made my way toward the front of the carriage. This carriage had been so graciously waiting for us when we entered Nyria through Cyx's portal. It was a weird gesture from Mother. I sneered; it's not like we needed a carriage. The timid laugh of the human cut through my thoughts. I couldn't help but flinch at the sound. *What could they have possibly said to make her laugh?*

My footsteps crunched along the pebbled ground, and I couldn't help but soak in my surroundings. The dense forest loomed around me, tall trees reaching for the sky and casting long shadows that seemed to dance beneath the suns' light.

Mother surely knew we had arrived, and while the

realization of this shouldn't have sparked my anxiety, it did. The fact she also conveniently had a carriage waiting for us left my stomach souring. It's not like we *needed* the carriage, because she knew Cyx could jump us across the realm efficiently enough. Maybe it was a little "I'm sorry for treating my only son like shit and sending you to a different realm" gift.

A bitter laugh escaped my lips as I closed my eyes. Surely, she knew we couldn't take the carriage for the entire journey. A gentle breeze slid around me as it rustled through the leaves, bringing with it the heavy scent of the surrounding land. Ehn truly was beautiful. The musty smell of damp soil mixed with the sweet scents of musk and bark lingered in my nose, a warm welcoming sense of familiarity crawling through me.

It was so good to be back.

I drank in the moment as much as I could, making the silent selfish decision from here on we would travel on foot to Hellebore. I didn't need random handouts from Mother, especially when I was sure there would be some caveat to it. That, or she'd likely throw it back in my face for being too lazy to use aura to bring the human to her immediately. No. She made me wait a century in the Human Realm. She could wait a few days for the human. I was going to savor this journey.

This would likely be a challenge despite perhaps using Cyx's portals here and there, but I had to admit I was looking forward to it. After a century in the hellscape that was earth, I would gladly greet even the scum of Nyria with opened arms.

One of the nedeer gave a loud huff as I came around to its side. I ran my hand down the dry, hair-like fur on its coarse thick column of a neck. I hadn't realized how much I had missed these giant beasts. The creature stood tall; its speckled earth toned frame wrought with dense muscle. I pressed my forehead to the creature's neck and buried my face into the nedeer's fur, giving it a silent "thank you" for towing our carriage. Seeing how the soilborn cared for and treated the animals of their realm was nothing short of horrifying.

A feminine voice rasped from behind me like the scrape of a rusty blade against stone. "We were being pulled by what? Giant pigs?"

I dropped my head from the beast and let out an audible, lengthy sigh.

Ah, so they decided to not cast her mouth.

Raising my head, I brought my hands to the reins of the giant creature's neck and slid the leather over its head, being careful to avoid its tusks and horns.

"Nedeer," I stated flatly.

"Well, they look like a boar and a ram had a big, ugly baby." The human snorted under her breath, as if I wouldn't hear the blatant insult to the creature.

I looked at the pair of nedeer in front of me. The beasts were nothing short of magnificent. Their beauty was in their strength and loyalty. I unbuckled the large leather strap from around its torso and looped the harnesses around my shoulder as I walked to the twin creature at its side.

"Did that insignificant human brain forget my order already?" I murmured. "Why are you speaking?"

The nedeer in front of me stood tall and poised, its chin

61

reaching just above my brow bone. The twisted moss green corkscrew-like horns protruded from their foreheads, easily towering over me by at least six inches.

I carefully removed the harness from the second creature, layering it on top of the one already draped over my shoulder. Moving to the front of the humble beast, I cupped its wide muzzle in my hands. Its smooth, black snout was perfectly centered between two wide-set tusks, and it pulsed with curiosity as it smelled the leathers on my chest. The creature lowered its head, adjusting its height for me, then it closed its obsidian eyes.

"You are dismissed," I whispered before releasing their muzzles. Once they strode into the dense foliage beside us, I turned my attention to the pest at my back.

She was filth. Human filth.

I didn't know if I could make it to Hellebore without killing her—whether for my own good or hers. Every sound that escaped out of her made me irate and curious. My wounded hands flexed, the skin there tight and tingling; clear evidence my aura had been working, sealing the wounds. A small part of me quietly hoped my body didn't heal itself too well. I wouldn't mind bearing her scars for eternity.

The sudden emotion startled me.

Just where was the attraction coming from?

Light began to crack at my fingertips as tiny electric currents danced across my skin, the golden light dancing between my fingers. Her eyes grew wide as she gasped. My teeth gritted together.

I knew she was aware I could kill her in an instant, if I so chose.

Good.

I wanted to drown in her distress.

I had hoped the show of my magic would be enough to quell her and shut her up. Unfortunately, it did not. My teeth ground together as I watched her jaw begin to work as she prepared to spew out another useless batch of words.

Before her lips could part, I flicked my right wrist at my side, pressing my pointer finger and thumb together. A thread of gold no thicker than a cobweb jolted straight toward the human. The light contrasted against the darkness of her mouth as it found its target, sizzling as it made contact and leaving behind a thin line of gold sealing her lips.

Her eyes widened, her hands—her unbound hands—shot up to her mouth as her filthy fingers prodded and pulled at her lips.

"Much better. See? You're far more tolerable when you shut that incessant mouth of yours."

Her cheeks turned scarlet beneath the dark grime coating her face. The sight sent a shiver of excitement down my spine even as she glared at me, her nostrils flared with anger. Messing with her in this manner was exhilarating.

I bent my knees to make my eyes level with hers and rested my palms just above my knees, the sparks smoking against my leathers. I caught my reflection in the full black saucers that overtook her caramel irises. She dropped her hands from her mouth and curled them into fists that hovered just below her ribcage.

This little rat was seething!

I had never seen such fight in a human. How brave of her to think she could do, what? Fight me? I choked back a laugh. It was almost cute. I raised my hand to her face and dragged a finger down her cheek, leaving a light pink burn in its wake as her lips unsealed. Her eyes were rimmed with tears; there was no doubt her flesh stung under my touch, but she didn't even flinch. I huffed, straightening.

Impressive little thing.

"Being the kind *prince* I am, I'll allow you to walk. If you try to run away, I'll cast your arms and legs just as I did with that little vermin mouth of yours and drag you by your scalp the entire way to Hellebore."

Her nostrils flared again, and I couldn't help but grin at her reaction. It was a shame Mother was going to carve that beautiful garnet heart out.

Withdrawing my aura, I turned to see Cyx and Seymour had been watching the entire time. Cyx's arms were now layered with the daggers he had previously stored away, the golden pommel of his longsword peeking above his head like a small halo. A satchel laid at his feet, and his eyes were fixated on me as he waited patiently for his next order.

Seymour, on the other hand, stood lazily beside the warrior and looked nothing short of bored. Annoyance played in his eyes as he looked at me and swatted at his sleeves in an attempt to alleviate the orange stains from before. I cocked an eyebrow at him.

Watch yourself, friend, I spoke to his mind.

We had always butt heads, even as younglings. It never

sat right with me how my own Mother seemed to favor him more than I. To have her favor someone that not only wasn't flesh and blood but wasn't even our kind. Perhaps it was my own jealousy, or my own insecurity. Regardless, he always remained loyal to me and at my side, despite it all.

He rolled eyes and shifted his gaze to everything but me.

I grabbed the satchel at Cyx's feet and shoved it into the sternum of the human. Despite her scowl, she complied and snatched it from my grip.

"You," I said with a sweet smile, cocking my head to the side and allowing my hair to fall into my eyes. "Congratulations on your new promotion to *mule*."

"Seymour, you will lead as our head scout. Stay ahead on the trail. I'll be right behind you. Cyx will remain at the rear with our new mule. Ehn is barren enough, but we can't afford any delays. We've already wasted enough time dawdling." I couldn't help the sense of unease.

Humans were a rare sight in this realm, and it would be hard to predict what we might come across. Original above, be damned, it was hard enough to predict if her body would even withstand the magic of this realm. She had no aura, and though she seemed astonishingly fine right now, there was still no telling what the aura of the lands may do to her as our journey continued.

Aura sustained all the beings in Nyria. It healed us, though some faster than others depending on the bloodline and how close a tie to the Ethereal a bloodline had. It also sustained us so our bodies did not need food or water and could last with minimal sleep if need be. But humans, they required those things. I didn't have the intention of setting up camp—though I planned to relish in the journey to Hellebore—and I couldn't waste time on menial soilborn things. Besides, there seemed to be enough fight within her. Perhaps she would hold just enough to make it to my territory.

Time worked differently in the Magic Realm. Though I'd spent nearly one hundred human years away, it was hard to gauge how things had changed here in that time.

I anticipated the river folk would not be pleased by my unexpected visit when we reached the waterway. It was not every day an exiled prince came home. In addition, some of Hellebore's allies would not take my arrival lightly. If that meant getting my hands bloody, so be it.

Ready? Seymour's voice chimed in my mind, pulling me away from my thoughts. I nodded.

Seymour rolled his neck and stretched his arms above him. He hadn't bothered to look directly at the human since I forced him into submission, and a part of me felt bad. I really didn't enjoy playing the role of a harsh leader, but I needed to uphold my title. If I showed weakness to one, I'd have to show weakness to all.

Seymour's skin rippled as if a stone were dropped into a pond. The sight of his skin contorting had always been both mesmerizing and disturbing. His frame shrank and bent unnaturally as his skin sagged in one place and sucked tight to the bone in others. I turned away at the sound of his muscle and tendons reshaping. The sound was sickening with wet noises accompanied by the pop of joints and gurgles that cascaded around him. It was a grotesque sight, witnessing a shapeshifter shift—even though I had watched him shift several times when we were young. Mother had whittled him into a weapon of sorts, but I never got used to it.

A short moment later, he took the form of a slender white cat and pawed his way from the heap of his former attire. Cyx kneeled and carefully gathered the discarded clothes, shoving them into the satchel the human was holding. A chuckle formed in my throat, but I pushed the reaction down as I noticed her eyes looking like they were about to pop out of her head.

Seymour sprinted ahead of us down the long stretch of road, kicking up mini plumes of orange dust. I settled for abandoning the carriage wholly; it would be stripped down to nothing for materials by other travelers, and I didn't want to waste time sifting through what we were leaving behind.

I set after him at a brisk pace, leaving Cyx to deal with the human.

CHAPTER 9
LUCILLE

"Walk," Cyx growled under his breath, his words floating in the air around me. My legs were frozen. I couldn't help but stare after Seymour as he sprinted down the stretch of road. I knew my face had paled, because the sight and sound of Seymour shifting had left my insides cold despite the three suns. My stomach churned as I thought about how I had petted and cooed at him. Something about *that* thought alone made my skin crawl more than what I had just witnessed.

A hand gripped my bicep, thick fingers pressing into my flesh through the sleeve of my sweater.

"I said, walk!" Cyx catapulted me in front of him.

My feet stumbled over the copper dirt, clouds wafting and sliding into my lungs. I stifled a cough into the crook of my elbow as I looked over my shoulder at Cyx. He lifted a finger in the air, twirling it to signify I should face forward.

I was so sick of these damn men.

The bag was too heavy to carry in one hand, and I could feel my coat brush against the back of my calves, the extra loose layer corralling heat around my legs—I was beginning to feel uncomfortably hot again. I was far past the point of a sweaty mess. Beads were already rolling down my face like tears. I groaned. The heat here was suffocating, and this walk already felt never-ending.

"So, what are you?" I asked as the silence grew uncomfortable. "The white-haired guy can change into a cat apparently, because that's a thing, I guess. What do you turn into?"

Silence.

"That kind of checks out, y'know? He's got that kind of—" I waved the satchel around. "That kind of vibe going on."

Silence.

"I know you can hear me. What?" I rolled my eyes, not that Cyx could see. "Did your boss tell you not to talk to me?"

"Prince," he stated in a low tone.

"Right, right," I replied. "You know, I didn't see you at his library. But Seymour was there—"

"Do you ever stop talking?" Cyx bit out.

The sound of dirt beneath my feet ceased and urged me to stop as though an invisible leash had bound me to him.

"Do you ever talk in general?" I quipped right back.

"You speak awfully comfortably for someone who was just abducted and brought to a different realm, soilling." His voice carried notes of distaste and annoyance.

I scoffed to ignore the strangeness of why I wasn't spiraling the way I should have been. It felt like a giant cage had formed around my brain since the moment I opened my eyes in the carriage. Sure, I freaked out when Sebastien was dragging me around like a tattered doll, but being here wasn't as off-putting as it should have been. Of course, the whole three suns and the person shedding their skin to turn into a cat situation was ludicrous, but…I felt a weird, numb calmness that I couldn't quite decipher.

"I didn't tell you to stop walking," Cyx snapped.

"I only stopped because you stopped," I countered. "Can you at least grab this bag for a sec so I can take off this coat? I don't know if you've noticed, but I'm not exactly dressed for the weather." I pivoted on a heel, the motion causing my head to spin slightly as my vision churned a swirl of green and orange.

"Please?" I cocked my head to the side, batting my eyelashes at him and pulling my bottom lip in a hair with my teeth.

"No, and whatever's wrong with your eyes, I encourage you to resolve it quickly. We have a long trek, and I have no intentions on carrying you."

I could feel my cheeks prick with embarrassment; it was worth a shot.

"Listen, brute. I don't know if anything goes on in that meaty,"—*Beautiful*— "head of yours, but it seems like whatever sick thing your boss—your *prince*—has planned for me, he needs me alive. I don't know what type of *thing* you are, but I can't walk miles in a full coat and sweater in this heat." My breath came rapidly as I sucked hot air and dust.

His jaw flexed. His eyes fell to the soiled coat that hung off my elbows, and he loosened a breath. I could tell I was beginning to get under his skin.

"The heat will dissipate the moment we get to the waterway," he replied.

"I will dissipate from this heat before we get to the waterway," I countered.

A small exhale escaped him, his nostrils flared with what I assumed was frustration. He closed the gap between us with two long strides, his hand simultaneously drawing out a small cobalt dagger from his arm.

"Turn," he commanded.

A smirk played on my lips as I gave him my back, feeling the pressure of his dagger on my coat as he began to saw at the fabric. Seizing the opportunity, I clutched the satchel between my two fists and turned on my heel. With as much force as I could muster, I thrust the sack into his face.

The contents felt hard and heavy, and I doubted it would be enough to knock him out, but *maybe* it would be just enough to give me a chance to run for it. I didn't know where I'd run to, exactly—I'd wager straight into the brush beside us where those beasts had gone. The carriage must be only half a mile away. I wasn't sure if I could make that, but I could definitely take cover in the trees. And from there? I'd figure it out. I'd be damned if I let these men take me.

Unfortunately, my blow was met with a calmly raised hand. He grabbed the satchel before it made contact, his face solemn and unreadable. I quickly released the bag and darted to his left toward the forest.

Something hard crashed into the back of my head, the sound of clattering objects following the blow. I faltered a few paces. The forest was so close. If I could just—

My foot slid beneath me, and I slammed to my knees. From the corner of my eyes, I saw leather clad legs beside me. Did he seriously just trip me?

Vials, pouches, and a few small leather notebooks were scattered next to his feet.

He threw the fucking satchel at me?

71

"Bold try." His monotone voice was dry.

I braced myself on all fours, panting in the copper dust, my sweat falling from my face and mixing with the dirt beneath me.

Cyx dropped to a knee beside me. "Care to try again, or have you learned you cannot best me, soilling?"

Soilling.

My fists clenched against the dirt.

"Throw that dirt in my eyes, and I will make a point to carve yours out and wear them as a necklace."

CHAPTER 10
SEBASTIEN

The suns' rays clawed me with molten talons. The trees that surrounded the path appeared to lean away from the vast stretch of dirt and folded in on themselves as if they were cowering from Ehn's heat. It had been too easy to forget what it was like under the three suns. We were in the southernmost portion of Nyria, and the heat here was volatile.

A subtle *thud* behind me caught my attention. I whipped around to see the human on all fours on the ground, Cyx kneeling beside her.

Shit.

"What happened?" I called out, jogging over to Cyx without taking my eyes off the human, who was surrounded by the contents of the satchel strewn around the dirt.

"She collapsed," he answered dryly. As he rose, he folded his arms over his chest.

I searched his eyes as I ran my hand through my hair, slicking it back with the sweat that had been collecting along my forehead. There was something hidden in his eyes I couldn't decipher. His loyalty to me knew no bounds, but he'd just lied to me.

I nodded and looked down at the human. She was still in clothes from her realm. I hadn't thought about that. She was still dressed for a cold, rainy day. Her sweater was beyond ragged, and along the back was clear evidence of where the stairs had repeatedly scraped against the fabric. A pang of remorse speared my chest. It was getting harder and harder to swallow these feelings.

The human rocked back, sitting on her heels.

"Stand," I ordered. Crouching, I noticed her vile scent. The stench of sweat, dirt, and old vomit clung to her clothes and skin, and I could almost taste the foulness on my tongue even as my throat constricted in an effort to block it out. "I gave you a command."

Was she ignoring me?

The human's knuckles turned stark white as her hands clenched around the dirt. She moved, angling herself to the side and cocking her hands back. Within the same breath, Cyx struck her, and she fell face first into the dirt.

I blinked, unsure of what had just happened except that Cyx had struck the human with the pommel of his sword. I wince, making the somber acknowledgment that I was sorely out of practice.

"You knocked her out?" The question was more of a statement. Of course he'd knocked her out. He had been my family's war leader prior to our banishment, and he could read an opponent's moves well before they were executed.

He secured the blade back behind his shoulders. "Sorry, My Prince. She was intending to throw the soil into your eyes. It hadn't seemed in that moment that you were prepared for the attack."

"No need for apologies," I mumbled.

Cyx nodded.

My hands moved on their own. The sleeve of my leathers caught against her sweat-soaked clothes and exposed a sliver of her skin, revealing where it had been scorched. It was painfully red, almost as if she had been held over a flame to cook. The sight nearly took my breath away. I had never studied a human body like this before. Granted, between all the time I had had on my hands and the number of humans I had captured, I really should have.

For a moment, I began to wonder about the corpses I had left behind. There had to be countless bodies beneath the dirt of the estate. I shudder at the thought but ultimately let the memory fade into the abyss of my mind.

I'd known they were fragile from my dealings with them on earth, but I didn't know they were so fragile that the Nyria's suns could practically cook them.

Without thinking, I pulled the back of her sweater up to her shoulders, piling the material at the base of her sweat slicked neck, exposing her sun bitten skin.

Her wounds from the library were not nearly as bad as I had anticipated. In fact, they appeared completely healed. Her healing flesh implied the aura of this realm did impact humans, but perhaps not in the way I had assumed. It seemed to speed up her healing process—almost in the same manner that it did for us. But her back was still a collage of fresh and angry red burns of varying severity. Small blisters clustered together in some areas, while others were more saturated and swollen. The pattern of the blisters matched the gaps in her top. My eyes hovered on two obscure marks slanted across her shoulder blades, separated by her spine, mirroring one another. I could feel my aura stir as I stared at them.

Hmph.

It was astonishing she had made it this far without showing an ounce of the pain she had endured from the suns.

"Do you plan to heal her, Prince?" Cyx interrupted my thoughts, angling his body above us to provide a broad section of shade.

I tensed. *Did I plan to heal her?*

The air around Cyx shifted as his aura began to concentrate around him.

"I can portal us to straight Hellebore, if you wish," he said with caution.

I held my hand up, opening my mouth only to close it. I could have had Cyx portal us to my land the moment we arrived, foregoing the carriage completely, but this apprehension I'd felt since setting foot back in this realm had created a mental block within me. Something nagged at my soul. Was it the thought of facing Mother after all this time? I *could* chalk the feeling up to simply wanting to savor my return to Nyria before rushing straight to Hellebore, but something within me knew neither were true.

What was it? What was I so hung up on?

I released the damp fabric and searched through her matted hair, where I knew she had a gash. That wound had been fully healed as well. I dragged a finger across her neck, locating the spot on her throat just under her jaw and feeling the soft thrum of her strong pulse.

I *could* heal the burns, but it was only her heart that

mattered, the husk that contained it didn't matter so long as that organ in her chest continued to beat. She'd likely have scars, but I couldn't let that matter to me. She'd be just fine. The land would continue to care for her, and that would be enough. It would have to be.

I was avoiding his question, stalling.

"We're close enough to the waterway. Mahni will already know of our arrival when we get into Amisa, and he will likely have a room ready for us. We'll just keep her in the room temporarily."

That perceptive beast of a King, I was going to have to pay him a visit. If anyone could bring insight into what was causing these bizarre reactions my heart was having to this human, it would be him.

Cyx eyed me skeptically. "She'll need to eat, so when we arrive in the city, I'll get her food."

"She's fine."

Silence hung thick in the air.

"I can portal us to—" Cyx began.

"I am aware you can portal us!" I barked. "The jump here subdued her for damn near a whole day. She needs to be able to function, unless *you* intend to carry her." I stood; my annoyance having created an electric current of aura through my veins.

Cyx stiffened at my sudden outburst—he'd received worse from me, but it always sprung a leak of guilt in my heart to snap at him. He meant well, only offering to portal us close to Hellebore out of convenience solely for me.

I reached out and placed a hand on his stiff shoulder.

"Listen. You have served my family well for centuries. It is on me to correct our wrongful banishment. Portal to Seymour, figure out where that insect is—I don't feel like searching for him myself. I'll be fine. I'll be right behind you."

His eyes bounced between mine. I knew he valued the compliment, but I also knew he hadn't liked my avoidance of his question—and I didn't like that he had lied to me. He nodded swiftly, a flash of relief dancing across his features for a second before taking a step back. He closed his eyes and tilted his chin toward the bright sky, nostrils flaring as he inhaled deeply.

I watched as he unfolded his arms, thick tendrils of purple smoke lacing between his fingers. The dusty, orange soil beneath his boots turned midnight. Smoke curled around him tightly, embracing him like a lover before it cascaded down to pool at his feet. In an instant, the hole of a portal swallowed him and left fresh, evenly placed dirt behind. Unlike Seymour's shifting, watching portal magic never got old.

It was safe to assume Seymour had made it to the border of Amisa. I didn't want to risk—or waste my energy—carrying her. I *could* fly, but my wings had always made me self-conscious. Fae royalty had wings. Well, historically we royals were *allowed* to have wings. When the Ethereal created this realm, the original "people" here had been products of population overflow in their realm—but history had shown that Ethereal who were born weaker were the ones who had been sent here.

As a youngling, I was taught when Nyria was separated into territories nearly a millennium ago, each sector had a royal figure. At the time, it was determined those who had the strongest traits and blood connection to those in the Ethereal Realm were deemed royal. That test had since been lost to time. To my knowledge, the strongest populations and primary royal figures were typically Fae. The part of history that always stuck with me was that *royalty*—and royalty alone—kept their wings. Lesser Fae had their wings removed at birth. It was a gruesome fact to learn as a youngling, and had haunted the back of my brain since.

I always held respect for lesser Fae—the common workers, we were all the same. The only difference was in bloodline and strength. The purer the bloodline, the stronger the being.

A sigh escaped my chest as I straightened my spine and pressed my shoulder blades together in an attempt to loosen up. The last time I had used my wings was when Hellebore was at war with Myrnen. The war had been beyond hellish.

Mother had always been a fiend for power. Whether it was more power, more land, or more bodies to employ for whatever she seemed fit. Just more. Whatever she wanted, she'd used my father as her pawn, her talons ever burrowing into his soul. It was hard to tell if the things he did for her were out of love or out of fear.

The Battle of Myrnen.

That utterly senseless war had raged for days over nothing. She had eradicated nearly an entire species with that war, and as the gold-hearted folk of Myrnen fell, so did my father.

It made sense my comrades and I had been exiled. If I had been more aware of my surroundings, my father might have still been alive. If I had just paid a little more attention, or even if I hadn't been so arrogant as to send Cyx and Seymour away during the heat of battle, he would still be here. Hellebore's *king* would still be here, and I was sure I could have snapped him out of whatever hold Mother had on him. Without him, there was no telling what she's done during all this time, especially because territories weren't fond of having queens as rulers. There was a part of me that was full of so much regret; despite knowing it wasn't my fault he died. It was war, and I had been so young.

I shook my head in hopes of shaking the thoughts away. I needed to stop with the downward spirals—they ate me alive, but I couldn't seem to quell them completely.

The suns were almost setting, the smallest one sitting highest in the sky while the other two slowly tucked themselves into the horizon. Like most places, Ehn could be nightmarish after dark. But here, and where we were headed, the lush green and orange-filled forests of Ehn could be unforgiving.

The Ethereal had done an interesting job in forming all the different territories. Half of the time, none of it made sense. Ehn was lush and hot. Amisa, on the other hand, was nothing more than an arid desert which, surprisingly enough, was less hot despite the barren land.

I chuckled to myself as I thought about how the people of Amisa weren't much different from trapdoor spiders in a sense. Hiding in their hole of a city beneath the sand, only to emerge at night when the moon gave them cover from the creatures above.

Though their cities were beautiful, their inhabitants were nothing short of bloodthirsty creatures. I always found that to be ironic. The beings here of Amisa were outcasts —absolutely cluttered with unfortunate souls. I rubbed my face with both hands. I was stalling.

I glanced around out of habit, knowing I was alone except for the human. The Ehn forests were void of life except for small critters or other travelers looking for solace. But the thought of someone watching my wings erupt made my stomach twist anxiously.

I inhaled slowly as I pulled my shoulders inward slightly, the unused muscles spasming before the subtle sound of tearing leather filled my ears. I felt my wings spread out to their full length, flexing as if they had a mind of their own. The suns warmed every feather, their darkness absorbing the light hungrily. The wings flapped in my peripherals, the long black feathers looking like they were carved from the night sky. The Hellebore family, *my family*, had obtained the name the "Family of Crows" because our wings looked as though they were composed of hundreds of giant, crow-like feathers. They were an intimidating sight, and to my knowledge, my family held the largest wings in Nyria, allegedly rivaling those of the Ethereal's. Deep down, I knew that also played a role in my self-consciousness. It didn't seem fair.

I crouched at the side of the unconscious human and scooped her into my arms. Seymour's aura was incredibly easy to track. I cast my aura out around me like a mental net and waited for that internal ping to notify me of his exact whereabouts. The familiar sense of Seymour's aura hummed in the back of my head, giving me a sense of which direction to head in.

Good. He was only a few miles away.

The flight there would be brief. I readjusted the human in my arms, though I could have easily held her in one arm if needed. I gave my wings one last flex, sending large clouds of orange into the dusk air around us. With a small bend of my knees, I launched us into the sky.

The speed was alarming, at first. I had forgotten what this had felt like. Adrenaline rioted within me, my heart pounding erratically. I encouraged my wings to beat against the air in long, strong strokes—higher, higher. The forest shrank as we neared the clouds above. I forced my wings straight out and glided along the air, feeling the light of the smallest sun warm the feathers, savoring the feeling—I finally felt free.

The royal blood that coursed through my veins electrified, the primal part of me reveling in this powerful blessing of flight. It was intoxicating. I allowed myself one moment before slowly dropping from the air. The sensation of my descent pulled me from my euphoric high as I searched internally for that sense of Seymour, allowing my wings to take control as they beat mindlessly against the wind.

I angled my body parallel with the ground below and held the girl close to my chest. That peculiar pull in my heart resurfaced as I adjusted her so she nestled closer and I could shield her from the harsh winds. The ground beneath blurred as my mind slipped into the wonder of the girl in my arms.

If she were Fae, I would have sensed it. That, and we wouldn't even be here right now. She felt and smelled human. With no detectable aura, she had to be a different creature. But those marks on her back were only present on beings whose wings had

82

been removed. There was no reason she would bear similar scars.

The primary species of Nyria were shapeshifters and Fae, but all beings had a well of aura into which they could tap. Even the smallest creatures of Nyria had their own minuscule holds of aura, and lesser demons would occasionally leak over from the Ethereal Realm had their own energy that twinned aura, and though it was significantly darker, it was a type of aura nonetheless.

My mind flickered to the Ethereal themselves. If we didn't know about their realm, they would have been nothing more than myth. They never visited either of the realms they created, so as far as I was concerned, there was no chance she was an Ethereal. Nonetheless, if this girl in my arms had an ounce of aura, I would have sensed it.

Seymour's aura grew turbulent, pulling me from my thoughts. I scanned the flashes of forest below, honing in on every speck on the ground with precision until the vibrant forest of Ehn was abruptly cut off by the harsh border of Amisa—and not too far from the borderline, I spotted the waterway. Wind rippled through the sands like invisible fingers dragging across its surface, undisturbed by the dark shapes of the shadows cast by the suns.

Movement caught my attention, and I tucked my wings close to my frame, spearing for the ground. I wound my arms around the limp human and cradled her head into the crook of my neck just as my feet slammed into the peak of a dune. A burst of sand erupted around us as I spotted Seymour, but the girl stayed unconscious. He was fighting at the bottom of the dune.

His grunts and calls filled the air as I dropped my wings,

letting their weight rest against the sand.

"Cyx, the wings—now!" Seymour's voice was a primal roar that seemed to vibrate the air around him. His hand plunged deep into the bare chest of a creature, his muscles bulging beneath the linen from the effort. Blood seeped down his forearm, soaking into the white fabric of his sleeve. The creature threw its head back in agony, a blood-curdling scream tearing from its lips.

Seymour didn't hesitate. He impaled the creature with his other hand. I could hear the wet squelch as his claws dug deep into the gaping wound. It attempted to raise an arm to fight off Seymour, but the creature was already mutilated beyond recognition, its arms having been shredded into ribbons from the elbow down, its tendons and muscle hanging over the merlot-red sand. I watched eagerly as Seymour adjusted the angle of his hands in the chest cavity when red leather wings erupted from behind the creature.

A lylan?

"I have her heart. Get the damn wings before she regenerates! Original above, man, help me out here!" Seymour roared again.

The lylan wore only a garment made of a sheer white fabric that hung loosely between her legs. Her red, leathery wings flapped frantically as she made another pitiful, futile attempt to escape. Blood flowed like a river from the wound in her chest, a scarlet trail down her abdomen past her navel as it saturated the fabric at her hips.

What was a lylan doing out at this time?

They were strictly nocturnal, and even dusk was too early

for them to be out. Lylans were a bit of a gray area when they came to Nyria; often referred to as tainted Fae, they earned the moniker from their dark and malicious aura. Everyone knew Amisa's nightlife was a beacon for these succubus-like demons who usually preyed on the heartbroken and crestfallen, seducing them to their own demise. It was baffling to see lylan out at this time of day. I squinted at the creature, realizing there was something off about it. It looked like it had three pebbles lodged between its eyes.

Odd.

The lylan's soulless eyes darted up to me as if it could sense my scrutinizing stare—only, it wasn't looking at me. It was looking at the human.

"Please, *please!*" she screamed, her body convulsing as thick globs of blood fell from her mouth with each word. Her crazed eyes scanned the girl's body in my arms. "I'll give you my blood! As many vials as you wish!"

Was she talking to me or to the human?

"Please," the lylan continued, a bloody arm rising in our direction as if to beckon us over. "Anything! You can take my blood! Or please, I can offer you secrets!"

Cyx, who had been standing idly by, took three long strides toward the demon and placed one hand on each wing. A wet rip followed a symphony of cracks as her wings ripped from her flesh with ease.

The lylan screeched as tears poured from her eyes, and blood gushed to pool around her feet. Seymour let out a low growl as he jerked his elbows back. A glistening heart pumped between

85

his bloodied hands. The lylan fell to her knees, then face first into the hot sand. Her body immediately began disintegrating, turning into charcoal flakes in the air.

Seymour stared at the pulsating organ between his hands, his eyes gleaming with a feral hunger. Cyx dropped the fading wings over the lylan's decaying body. A disgusted look crossed his usual complacent face as he walked to Seymour, who looked like he was about to bite into the heart as if it were an apple.

Cyx swatted the organ from Seymour's hands, and it rolled along the sand before Cyx threw a dagger through its center. Warning laced his eyes as he looked at the shapeshifter.

We had been back in Nyria for less than a day, but they had already readjusted nicely. I didn't feel the need to question them; my comrades would always do what they deemed necessary to clear the path for me—always. Pride formed in my heart, but I kept my face solemn as I took in the sight of my friends. Cyx said nothing as Seymour wiped his hand on his thighs, his claws already reverting to their unshifted state. If he had eaten the demon heart, that could have been the end of us all. I'd have to deal with it later.

My wings retracted, cracking as they nestled back into the spots between my shoulder blades. I wouldn't need them, because the waterway was the sole entrance to the nocturnal city. Cyx began the process of preparing a portal, anticipating my request. I had never cared for Amisa or the creatures it harbored at night, and the thought of them had a shiver sliding down my spine as images of shadow-taunts flashed through my mind.

"The waterway," Cyx stated our next destination.

I trudged through the blood-soaked sand and shifted the human to cradle her in one arm—she hadn't stirred from the commotion, and part of me was glad for it. I rested my other hand on Cyx's shoulder as Seymour did the same, looking exhausted and filthy as he also rested his head on the Portal Mage. Cyx's discomfort was evident as he subtly shifted his shoulder in an attempt to shake Seymour off.

I gave in to the chuckle that formed in me, my chest bouncing the human body softly off mine. To be fair, I also felt uncomfortable when Seymour touched me.

Seymour yawned as we slipped through the ground into the smoky glow of the portal. "I could use a shot of Fae-kiss."

The world melted away in translucent tendrils of amethyst.

We spawned at the edge of a ravenous stream that was a rage of volatile blue. Getting into the city was always a death trial of sorts, a sick jest. But that was the territory the king had always been best known for. Was he a good warrior? Not by any means. Could he hide an entire population in plain sight for centuries? Sure, he's a tricky bastard. Did he love sick games? Absolutely.

Cyx unsheathed a dagger from his arm and ran the blade across his palm. Stepping onto the bank, the water cut around his thighs as he held his hand over the temperamental flow and squeezed. His knuckles whitened at the force as a thin stream of blood fell into the hungry waters.

The trick was to feed the spirited waters consenting blood. Though it was simple, not everyone knew about it. There were plenty who wandered into the malevolent stream in search of the city's entrance without the knowledge of what to do. Those poor souls were lost to a rather gruesome death, preyed upon by the creatures who dwelled in the waterway—kelpies, wraiths, and furred waterbed beasts with fangs as long as a man's arm.

There was a time in my youth when the king would hold bicentennial exhibitions. He would create a pit in the farthest corner of the city—an underground coliseum where the whole area was layer upon layer of illusion. Contestants were tasked to run through the curated labyrinth, chased by their own nightmares brought to life. Nothing was ever as it seemed in Amisa, but if you played the king's game—and played it well—he'd grant you a reading. His aura lent him a massive reserve to configure elaborate, tangible illusions, and it could be used to show a person's future. He was so powerful, yet he always chose to squander it all.

The water's irritated blue surface calmed where it mixed with the blood, a golden circle growing from the size of a seed into a wide, circular spread of aureate light, the faint hue of steps forming at its center and tunneling down. The current rushed around the stagnant spot, lapping over the sides of the golden cylinder slicking the steps. Cyx was the first to step foot inside, gauging the entrance for foul play or anything askew. Still standing beside Seymour on the bank, I placed a hand between his shoulder blades and gave him a small shove.

"You're up next." The words left my lips dryly. Seymour soundlessly followed Cyx, taking the ghostly stairs with caution. I cast my senses out around me for good measure as they made their way down. This bank cut through the rough middles of the desert with nothing but dunes of scorched sandy terrain surrounding us, but after what I'd witnessed with the lylan, I would not take any chances of anyone hindering my delivery of this damned heart.

I heaved the human over my shoulder, her boney hip digging into me as I stepped after Seymour. The moment my feet hit the step, the entrance shrank in on itself, sealing us into the tunnel. Soft light permeated through the weeping sand walls, accompanied by the pulse of electronic music.

"The walk to the city should be brief enough," I declared as we continued down the tunnel.

A small gold scroll appeared just ahead of us. I pushed past Seymour, who cursed me under his breath as I snatched the floating parchment and shook it open.

"I knew that old hog would know the moment we stepped foot in his territory," I grumbled, crumpling the glowing parchment in my fist and scoffing.

I turned to two men behind me. "Reighn Hotel. You are both to head straight there. I'll find food for the human. Cyx, make rounds around the hotel." I paused and narrowed my eyes at Seymour. "*You*. Stay with the human. If she wakes up, do not let her leave. Do not let anyone see her. Just get her into the hotel unnoticed. We don't need anyone seeing we brought a human into the realm."

Seymour's jaw ticked at the order, a small fire igniting behind his eyes—he had been more defiant since we got back to Nyria. I couldn't help but cock my head at him, narrowing my eyes at his defiance. My jaw clenched, knowing I should reprimand him, but the human wasn't awake. I had no need to put on the show of the "royalty" for her. I signaled for him to come to me with a jerk of my head. Reluctantly, he walked forward. I shoved the limp human into his arms.

"Are you good?" I questioned.

Seymour glanced at me and tossed a moonlight lock behind his shoulder, flashing me a grin. But I wasn't convinced. Something had been off about him since we had entered the realm, causing his already insufferable catty attitude to inflate.

"Never better," he winked.

I had no choice but to trust him, after all, we had been by each other's side for centuries. I had been his first friend when my family took him in.

"Do not disappoint me," I warned, and chalked his odd attitude up to him settling back into his aura and being back in the realm.

"*Do not* come back with trash," he mimicked my voice, and flashed me a white smile as he gripped the girl.

My teeth snap together, he had always known how to get under my skin. The sound of my own voice coming from his mouth sent a ripple of annoyance through me. I had *always hated it* when he'd mimic my voice.

Original above, we didn't have time for this right now!

Surely someone, some*thing*, somewhere would take heed of my return to Nyria. If the king had sensed me this fast, there was no doubt in my mind others had as well—if they hadn't heard from someone else first. Between the royals, this entire realm was a rumor mill. I was confident word spread immediately after our arrival, just as it had with my banishment. In all fairness, it *was* uncommon for someone to be banished when the preferred method of punishment—by nearly all territories—was execution.

"Mimicking me? *Really?*" I snarled and stepped toward him.

Seymour squared his shoulders. I brought my index finger up to his forehead, sparks already crackling at the tip as irritation simmered my blood.

I jabbed my finger between his eyes as my aura smoked against his skin. "Watch."

"Your." *Jab. Tss.*

"Repulsive." *Jab. Tss.*

"Tongue." Sparks rained down onto the girl.

"Before I cut it out and make you wear it like a collar, you incessant worm," I smirked.

I left my forefinger on his forehead, my fingertip sinking a few millimeters into his flesh. His nostrils flared at the pain.

"Stop wasting time acting like a youngling and *get moving.*" I turn my back to him and wait for him to walk ahead of me.

"I am *so* relieved to know that old trick still irritates you the same as when we *were* younglings," he laughed over his shoulder.

I eyed Cyx, exasperated.

"He will be the death of us all," I sighed hiding my amusement with Seymour.

Whether or not it was proper of me as a Prince to let

anyone speak to me the way he did was not a care of mine. Seymour knew I held immense guilt in my heart for what he has been through. I could withstand a bit of disrespect here and there.

CHAPTER 11
LUCILLE

It was like millions of warm fireflies were swarming inside me, the waves of warmth pushing and pulling through me like a lazy tide. The sensation began in my toes, slowly sloshing its way up my calves, my thighs, lower back, climbing up my spine vertebrae by vertebrae. My ribcage felt swollen with this immense, but comforting pressure, as the toasty feeling worked its way up the base of my skull, cradling my brain for a moment before it ebbed its way down the same path. This feeling repeated itself several times. It feels so nice, so cozy...

"Hu—or uh, Lucille? Can you hear me?"

My brain was foggy, and I didn't want to open my eyes to see who had spoken to me. I nestled my face into the soft fur that my head rested on. I wanted to go back to the fireflies.

A gentle hand rested against my forehead and pushed the hair from my face, then something cold and rough touched my lips. Wetness slowly coated my dry skin as liquid dribbled. I slid the tip of my tongue out and ran it between my lips, catching the droplets of liquid.

"Come on, Lucille. Your body needs more than that. Can I sit you up?" asked the voice.

I didn't want to leave the softness of the fur. Was I dreaming? Was all of what had happened some twisted nightmare?

Sedona Jessie

I grunted in response to the stranger's question—not quite a yes or a no. A hand slid underneath my shoulder and gingerly moved me until I was in an upright position. *Rude.* I didn't want to be sitting. I wanted to be back in the soft, cozy warmth.

It was like the fog in my brain had taken over my eyeballs, because I felt so sleepy. The rough, cool ridge of the mystery vessel wiggled gently between my lips again. Cool liquid rushed through my teeth and coated my tongue before it slid down my throat. Something primal came over me from the sensation and taste, like my body has been starved for years, and this liquid was what it longed for. I reached my hand up and fumbled blindly for the vessel until I felt the rough leather on my palms. I opened my mouth to take long gulps. I wasn't even thirsty, but the liquid was heavenly.

I opened my eyes and wiped my mouth with the back of my hand. I was in a room—a weirdly luxurious room. I had been laying on what looked like a chaise lounge, which was surprisingly comfortable. I ran my fingers along the rich, purple velvet covering the cushion and placed my hand on the large, round brown pillow that still had an indent from my head—it was the softest material I had ever felt.

"Soft, right?" Startled, I turned toward the voice and suddenly remembered I was not alone. *Seymour.*

He sat cross-legged on the floor in front of me and casually leaned back onto his elbows. His clothes were different; his previous linen attire was replaced by rich, emerald silks embroidered with iridescent threaded patterns snaking around the collar of his shirt. His white hair was tossed up in a messy bun

94

with strands of moonlight falling loosely around his face as he smiled at me. The light in his eyes was breathtaking, but I looked away, not wanting to stare for too long. Instead, I examined the room.

Several gorgeous lounge chairs were scattered around. While some were nestled against walls, others were propped by curtained windows. Everything was the color of the richest gemstones. Satin panels of white fabric streamed from every wall in the room, tapering as they met an astonishing chandelier hanging at the center of the ceiling. Its light was uneven, as if it wasn't a light bulb, but a living thing that illuminated the space. Crystals in the shape of tears hung from the tendrils of the chandelier, glittering as they sent cascades of miniature rainbows throughout the room.

Seymour spoke carefully, his cadence delicate as if he were trying to coax a scared cat out from under the bed, tilting his head ever so slightly. "Do you want to take a look outside? Maybe stretch your legs a bit?" He leaned forward as he spoke, placing his elbows on his knees, propping his perfectly chiseled chin on his fist.

I weighed the offer. He *was* the only one out of this group of assholes who had shown me any form of kindness, but what if this is some weird test or a trap? Flashbacks of the sight of him turning into a cat played in my mind like a reel.

Literally. A. Damn. Cat.

Was this kindness a ploy? This pretty white-haired *thing* sitting at my feet looked innocent enough, but he could definitely kill me with ease.

"I won't hurt you. You're safe with me. I know that sounds like a lie, but I promise I have no ill intentions toward you." He lifted his hand and drew an *x* over his heart.

He extended a hand toward me as if to place it on my knee, but I recoiled, snapping my eyes shut and flinching on instinct, terrified a claw would burst through his flesh.

He chuckled and dropped his hand. "Listen, if I wanted to kill you—if *we* wanted to kill you—you would have been dead the moment you stepped foot in Bas's estate back in the Human Realm."

As if *that* would reassure me. I released the tension in my muscles, but didn't dare relax. Just enough to not cramp up in case I needed to try to make a run for it.

"Where are the others?" I asked. My voice was so quiet, I cleared my throat and tried again. "Where are the other men?"

I wasn't sure I wanted to know the answer to the question as unease formed in my stomach when I noticed it was just me and Seymour here on our own. My words felt thick, but at least the fire in my throat disappeared at some point along with the aches and pains from before. My whole body felt great, actually.

"Bas is out finding you something to eat. Cyx is...I'm not sure where he went off to, exactly, but he's patrolling. Boring, I know. He kind of just does his own thing, which leaves me on Luce watch!" Seymour winked, his teeth on full display with that smile again.

He stretched his long legs out and tucked his feet under the chaise I was on. I didn't care for the nickname *Luce,* but it was better than *human.* Hell, it was way better than *soiling* or *filth.*

I stared at the man in front of me who seemed pleasant to talk to and to be around. The no-asshole-ness was refreshing, but weren't most killers deceptive like this? All those true crime stories seemed to say so. For the most part, something in me could tell there was no ill intent behind his words.

I hadn't been too concerned about where Cyx was, but Sebastien, on the other hand? No part of me wanted to see him again. Ever. Let alone eat anything he brought back with him. I couldn't stand that brat or the way he looked at me as if I were shit on the bottom of his shoe. As if *I* were inconveniencing him by being here. Like I even had a choice in the matter.

"Are you sure you don't want to look outside? Amisa is beautiful at night. If you thought the trio of suns was cool, just wait until you see our moons. We're fortunate, being in the middle realm. We get to enjoy the three realms of the solar system simultaneously. It's a treat, really." he leaned toward me again. "Mahni's aura is damned impressive, too. Do you like cities? Clubbing? I can see if Bas would let us check out one of the clubs here. Original above, I miss the clubs. You know what? Maybe when one of them returns, I'll find us some Fae-kiss. I don't know how it would affect a human, but it's a damn good time. Tasty drink, too!"

Between more talk of realms, clubbing, and whatever the hell Fae-kiss was? This guy was really trying to be buddy-buddy with me.

"Aura?" I asked, trying to seem like I had been listening as I brought the vessel back to my lips.

The corners of his eyes crinkled. "Sure, yeah. That makes

97

sense. It all probably sounds crazy to you. Aura is exactly how it sounds, for the most part. The internal glow of our soul that shines outwards. It's our force of energy—magic. It's largely different from being to being, but all the same, nonetheless. We can rally our internal energy and manipulate it."

"Magic," I echoed. This guy was a straight up nut.

He gave a small nod as he held up his hand. The skin along his fingertips convulsed and rippled, his fingers snapping sickly as they morphed into three long, hooked talons. I could feel my face twist with disgust.

"I know." He laughed at my reaction. "It's not pretty. Mine isn't, at least when watching the shift happen. But my aura manipulates and alters my DNA. Allows me to take the form of anything. If I've seen it, I can become one. Hurts like a bitch, but ya get used to it. You know?"

No. No, I did not know.

"So…You can shift into other people?" I asked. I needed to take advantage of his chatty mood and maybe unravel the reason I was here, and what the hell he kept rambling about.

He pulled his lip inwards and chewed lightly as his skin changed back into its normal state. "Technically, but that's a big rule for my people. We don't do that. That's—"

"There's more of you?"

Sadness dropped across his eyes like a sheet. "There was."

"Three realms?" I asked, changing to a different topic as guilt nudged me.

"Three realms," he parroted. "The Ethereal Realm, Magic

Realm, and the Human Realm. They all kind of overlap, but it's pretty hard to cross planes unless you're Ethereal or a strong Portal Mage."

"And we are in the…Magic Realm right now? What's in the Ethereal Realm? More things like you and your friends?" The corners of his lip twitched downward at the word *things*.

"I'll break it down for you." He repositioned himself, as if sitting still was the last thing he wanted to do. "The Ethereal are essentially the creators of the realms. Their whole realm is composed of Angels— think of them as gods, I guess. Cross breeding is strictly forbidden there, so the vast majority there are Angels and demons. But they created demons to provide *balance* to their realm. You can't have the good without the bad, or whatever that phrase is. Basically, our realm—Magic Realm—was created as an overflow realm, but in reality, it ended up being more of a trash can for their realm, where they'd send weaker Ethereal bloodlines here. Over millennia, some bloodlines evolved into other types of beings through cross breeding within this realm, mixing families, and through whatever aura this realm was laced with. Shifters, pixies, Fae, a bunch of other beings too. Same with demons. We get the lesser ones for what I assume to be for the same reason—to provide balance."

He took a deep breath and checked I was still listening before continuing. "Our historians don't really know how we have the creatures we do, so the theory is some type of crossbreeding between demons and the other beings, blah-blah-blah, something about the land's reserve of aura. That doesn't seem likely to me, though. I'm sure the Ethereal just send us creatures they ended up not wanting after creation." His shoulders moved with a dramatic shrug, and he lifted his palms toward the ceiling to exaggerate the motion further.

My head spun with all the information. What kind of rabbit hole did I get dragged down?

"So, you're a Shifter?" If I could get him to talk about himself, I should be able to start scoping out a route out of here, too.

"I am." He clapped his hands together before tucking a loose strand of hair behind his ear. "You asked before if there were more of my kind. Well, there aren't many of us. There was this war centuries ago." His eyes glazed over and grew distant for a moment, as if he were recounting the war.

"Cyx and Sebastien?" I questioned, wanting him to keep talking as I scanned the room, noticing two doors.

"Cyx is a Portal Mage. He's our transport. He can't jump too far. Typically, he can do only twenty or so miles at time— allegedly. But if he doesn't use his aura for a long time, it collects, and he can make significantly larger jumps. That's how we made it back to our realm, I guess. He was also the Hellebore family's war leader, not that that really matters anymore. Bas loves titles." He rolled his head back and stared at the cascade of linen flowing across the ceiling.

"Bas is a Faery. A *royal Faery.* The Hellebore prince— *The Prince of Crows.*" He snorted. "Fae, are divided between royalty and lesser. Bas can give you the ins and outs on that, but royal Fae are the closest beings we have to Angels here. Their aura is vast and colorful, with each royal family having its own type that's distinctly their own and…" Seymour's voice trailed off as I tuned him out.

Two doors. I assumed one was a bedroom or maybe the bathroom. The other *had* to be the exit. I couldn't fully see out the window from where I sat, but I could see enough to know we were too high up for me to jump. I couldn't even spot any glass decorations or wall art that I could break to use as a weapon if needed. Everything in this room was plush—too plush.

"You don't like it?" Seymour asked, pulling from my scheming.

"Huh? I don't like what?" I didn't realize Seymour had moved from the floor and was standing off to the side, holding two long gossamer gowns. One was a light shade of pink, the other a dusty gray.

"I figured you might want to change out of what you're wearing. Your clothes are…Well." His lips formed a tight line, like he was trying to be polite and evade an unnecessary insult, but his face said it all. "Do you like either of them? If you want something else, I could run out when Bas comes back?"

Pink crept into his cheeks as if he were embarrassed by the offer. I looked down at my soiled clothes. My pants were riddled with holes and unknown stains from blood and vomit. I hadn't really had a moment to think of the state of my clothes, or even my hygiene for that matter. I shifted in my seat uncomfortably, growing self-conscious of my appearance and smell.

"Uh, the gray one is fine. When—why do you have dresses?"

Seymour's teeth flashed, and his shoulders relaxed as he walked over to me, tossing the pink gown onto one of the many chairs.

"Oh, don't worry about why. Worry about *which*. Gray is the final answer?" He waved the gown in the air. "The gray one has an open back, but it's modest. It should be easy enough to move in when we leave."

He looked between me and the gown.

"Uh, yeah—the gray one is fine," I mumbled.

"Amisa has the finest elixirs—bathing elixirs—by the way," he continued.

I knew I smelled, and that this encouragement to bathe and change was an offer made in kindness. With no consideration of my personal space, he grabbed my hands, pulled me up, and knocked the water vessel out of my grip, shoving the gown into my palms as a replacement.

"Come! I'll get you set up in the washroom and show you how things work here. Don't worry, I don't plan on watching you bathe or anything wild like that. I'm not into…" He gestured, waving his hand at my whole frame. *Oh? Rude?* I didn't know why that offended me, but it stung.

Reaching the door to the bathroom, I made a mental note the other door was, in fact, the way out. Seymour opened the door with a grand sweeping motion, beckoning me to follow him inside.

The bathroom walls were covered in a shimmering, jelly-like substance that undulated and reflected everything in the room in a warped fashion. The tiles on the floor were such a deep teal, they nearly resembled mini tidal pools bordered by delicate golden flowers which perfectly contrasted the soft ivory walls. It was honestly gorgeous.

The center of the room was a round bathtub which looked more like a small pool. It was surrounded by long porcelain counters holding numerous colorful liquids and stacks of fluffy towels. Everything in this bathroom seemed larger than life! Were the people here giants? The size of this room, compared to the room we had just left, didn't quite add up. Maybe it was all a part of the magic or *aura* or whatever he had rambled on about, or maybe it was some fancy perk of being with a *prince*—I sneered to myself at the thought.

My feet followed Seymour as he walked to a towering wardrobe, our footsteps echoing against the tiled floor. The wardrobe's dark iron surface gleamed in the bright light as I watched him with skepticism. With careful movements, he slowly opened its heavy doors, his body briefly disappearing within them. I tried to follow his hand with my eyes as he stretched his arm into the depths of the wardrobe.

I did not expect him to pull out two small lizards, their delicate bodies curled in lazy balls in the palms of his hands. Their scales glinted in the light, and cracks of burgundy webbed around their tiny, scaled bodies. One of the lizard's eyes opened as a little, pink tongue flicked out and swiped along a tiny beady eye.

My jaw dropped open as I stared at the groggy lizards in his hands. "Lizards? *Closet* lizards?" I burst out laughing, unable to contain my disbelief. "Did you seriously just pull lizards *out of a closet?* What the hell are you going to do with those?"

A smirk played on his lips at my reaction. He walked

carefully to the giant tub and plopped the lizards into the water, one at a time. I couldn't fight my curiosity even if I had tried, so I followed him and peered into the tub.

First, I was surprised to see it had already been filled with water. Second, the lizards.

I watched as they floated, stretching their scaly bodies before flicking their tails as though they were little propellers. Then, they rotated head down and plunged to the bottom where they curled into what appeared to look like little rocks. The water around them began to bubble and foam. As weird as it all was, they were pretty cute.

"They're warming the water?" I asked, watching the bubbles surface.

"Graavian salamanders. They're docile," Seymour offered as reassurance—as if that made it less weird to toss lizards into a tub. "A lot of lowborn use them to heat water and what not. Only the royals have enough aura at their disposal for things like that, so the rest just use what they have." He shrugged as I followed him to the counter below the gel "mirrors" surrounding us.

Seymour sifted through various vials before settling on two. One contained a shimmering mauve liquid, and another held clear liquid fizzed as he shook the vial. I trailed him as he led us back to the gargantuan tub, setting the mystery potions on the wide lip. He turned so abruptly my face stopped only a few inches from his chest. He took the gown from my hands and folded it nicely, placing it on the porcelain ledge next to the vials.

I remained completely still as Seymour gently brushed a stray, matted strand of my hair off my shoulder.

"Now, little human," he said with a soothing voice. "The clear liquid is soap. Pour it into the water and fully submerge yourself. It will work its magic on its own, as all of our liquids are specially crafted to do their jobs perfectly, so you don't have to lift a finger. Unless you want to." He winked down at me, and I felt heat rising into my cheeks. "And the mauve liquid is for your hair. Same routine. Pour it onto your strands and then submerge to rinse."

I nodded stiffly, suddenly feeling awkward from his flirtatious wink. Did he not gesture to my *whole* body earlier while telling me he wasn't into anything about me? I shoved the thought into the back corner of my brain. Worrying about whether this guy—this *thing*—found me attractive should not have even been a shadow of a thought. First, I'd take a bath. Then, I'd figure out how to escape.

He started toward the door, leaving me standing and watching him awkwardly. I glanced into the tub again, eyeing the lizards at the bottom.

"What about the lizards?" I called after him.

"Don't step on them! If it gets too hot, just toss 'em out the tub!" he called over his shoulder. "Oh! And don't touch the mirrors!"

I blinked after him, then shrugged.

I stripped my rank clothes off my body, letting them fall to the floor in a filthy pile, and kicked them toward the door. *It was nice of him to let me bathe. What a generous kidnapper.* Scoffing, I hoisted myself onto the shockingly cold—and tall—ledge of the tub. Everything here was so damn high up.

Lifting the vial containing the clear liquid, I popped the top off. The air immediately filled with a fresh and crisp scent, like a field of newly cut grass after a rain shower, with a hint of laundry soap. Seymour didn't specify how much to pour, so I measured with my heart and poured the whole vial. The water turned opaque, and the lizards at the bottom disappeared in the murky, soapy cloud as their bubbles mixed with the contents.

Slowly, I eased my legs over the edge, hovering them straight out in front of me, parallel to the water. Cautiously, I dipped one leg in, letting my calf hit the water first. It was a pleasant surprise that the temperature was perfect despite its simmering appearance. I lowered both legs into the tub in unison before sinking the rest of my body in.

I definitely had not taken into consideration how deep the tub was, because next thing I knew my ass hit the bottom. Thankfully, I couldn't feel any drowsy lizards beneath me.

The water was like thousands of firecrackers popping against my skin in a soothing way. Shifting my foot, I accidentally kicked one of the lizards. I froze, unsure if Seymour had told the truth when he said they were docile. Thankfully, the little amphibian didn't seem to mind, because it simply moved its body away from my leg. I imagined it was curling itself into a tight little ball.

I bobbed up and down, hopping from foot to foot in order to keep my chin above the water's surface, my lungs filling with the steamy air. The sizzling on my skin calmed, and I wiped the water from my eyes with one hand, grasping the ledge with my other to keep a steady hop.

Alright, next up, the magical two-in-one shampoo.

I snapped the top off of the mauve vial with one hand and was greeted with a soft floral aroma reminiscent of a lilac bush in full bloom. Dumping the contents onto my matted hair, I let it soak. The liquid felt thick and sticky, heavy on my scalp. I fought the small urge to lather the contents, curious to see if the shampoo would truly refresh my hair on its own.

I couldn't think of the last time I had actually taken a bath. Between all the moving around, I never seemed to live anywhere long enough to justify a bath when showers were much more efficient while I was constantly on the go. It was important to avoid settling too deeply in one place, and part of me always remained on the hunt for the *right* place.

A sad pang of realization crept its way into my heart. There was a good chance I would *never* find the right place—or even go back home. I hadn't allowed myself to wonder what these men wanted from me—or even more terrifying—what they wanted to do to me.

Letting myself sink deeper into the embrace of the water, I made more grand attempts to push the thought from my head. I took a few deep breaths, long and slow. Breathing deeply until my lungs could not take in any more air, holding it for a few counts, then exhaling until my lungs were depleted. Then repeat. Finally, I took one more deep inhale through my nose and plunged my head under the water. Using my free hand to run my fingers through my hair, I stayed under, encapsulated by the heat for as long as my lungs would allow.

When I surfaced, I could hear the faint cadence of voices

from beyond the door. The sweet sounds of my captors talking. I scoffed. They were probably planning on what to do with me after my bath. I felt like some prized cow awaiting slaughter, utterly vulnerable and helpless.

I released the ledge and relieved my legs from their duty of keeping me upright. Leaning back, I let the soapy water support my weight as I floated on my back. Between the moments of water flowing in and out of my ear canals, the voices grew more aggressive in their conversation.

CHAPTER 12
SEBASTIEN

I stood back, relishing the filth of the city. There was something so aggressively unroyal about being around such vile areas, and I loved it. It felt more fitting than relaxing in luxury. I couldn't stand the stark contrast between royal and non-royal beings in Nyria. The mighty, receiving their meals tailored to whatever they fancied, lived far more lavishly than necessary, while the rest lived like rats.

It was far too early in the morning for the streets to be muddled with party goers and fiends. The air felt heavy and sticky in my lungs, somehow sucking all the moisture from my insides. This city was a clusterfuck of disease on a good day. I scanned the neon-clad street where trash littered the sidewalks as a glitter painted posse traipsed through a pile of garbage, kicking it while filling the air with chortles. They looked haggard beyond repair, their lips dry and cracked, the corners of their mouths spattered with a bioluminescent film. Not much had changed since my last visit to Amisa a few hundred years ago.

My eyes spotted a small package of parchment.

That would work.

I reached the soiled pile with a few strides, locating a half wrapped crusted corner of bread peeking out of its parchment satchel. Snatching up the discarded bread, I shoved it in my pocket and rolled my neck, savoring the cracks that cascaded down my spine. Each pop released tension.

I didn't have any intention of wandering longer than necessary, as there was no telling what was going on back in the room. But I'd needed this break from her presence more than I cared to admit. The thought of her hurt—*really* hurt—made me feel ill and clammy for reasons I did not want to focus on. I needed to focus on keeping her stable. That was all that mattered—not her well-being. She just needed enough fuel to keep that precious heart pumping.

I could feel the wall in my brain as my mental fist beat against it. *Could Mother really resurrect my father?*

That would go against everything I'd ever learned about this realm, but I supposed nothing was truly impossible, unless of course the Ethereal deemed it fit to tamper with the realm. No one to my knowledge had ever tried to resurrect a being with a human heart. Just because it may have never been done, doesn't mean it couldn't.

Souls could live for millennia with ease, though only Ethereal were truly immortal. Well, that was a loose term. If they died, they could choose to return before their soul left their bodies. They could reanimate their own body, or they could return as a fresh soul. It was sickeningly generous, but it made sense for them as the creators of the realms, whereas everything else in Nyria disintegrated, their souls and bodies turning to ash. Once gone, gone for good.

I wanted to hold on to the hope that she could somehow do it—reanimate or return my father as a fresh soul—no matter how improbable it seemed in hindsight. But I knew deep down that mental wall standing tall in my brain was denial. My soul sighed.

That false hope was covering up something more vile, and sinister. I could feel it.

There was a part of me—bigger than the false hope—that was hungry for revenge. A part that wanted to flay her open in front of everyone in Hellebore.

What I really wanted, in my core, behind all the denial, was to tear her soul open and pour out all the power-hungry schemes and lies she had fed my people.

I wanted the entire realm to know she was the one who killed my father.

A heart for a heart.

CHAPTER 13
LUCILLE

It was impossible to know how long I had been floating there for, but by the look of my shriveled, waterlogged hands, I'd wager it had been a good thirty to forty minutes. The bickering outside the bathroom door had settled some time ago, and the air was now filled with the lowered voices of normal conversation pattern with hearty chuckles that seeped through the cracks of the door on occasion.

I wonder who the owner of the laughter was. It was so rich; it had to be Seymour. That guy always seemed to be in a great mood. Had he developed some resemblance of Stockholm syndrome when it came to Sebastien? Because that man was a whole asshole and a half. He seemed to have zero regard for anyone else, acting like all the lives around him were just meaningless tools, existing solely for fulfilling his commands. There was no wondering whether it was Cyx's happiness I heard, because I wasn't sure if I'd even heard him say a complete sentence that wasn't just in reply to something his *prince* said. The laugh had to have come from Seymour.

Lucky me to be taken by the world's most gorgeous, messed up men. Mr. Sunshine, Mr. Asshat, and Mr. Gloom.

By the time I decided it was finally time to get out of this bath, a low growl emitted from my stomach. I was surprised to only now feel hunger. It felt like I'd been with these men for ages, so I really hoped Sebastien would actually feed me. I planted my toes on the bottom of the tub, bobbing from foot to foot gingerly until I reached the edge, hoping I wouldn't accidentally step on one of the lizards. Placing two palms on the ledge, I hoisted myself up, eyeing a pile of fluffy towels sitting on the counter.

I was pleasantly surprised the change in temperature was comfortable rather than nipping at my skin as I pulled myself out of the tub, inch by inch. In fact, it felt like the air in here was getting incrementally warmer the more I left the water. I tossed each leg over until my dripping feet found the floor. It was safe to assume the room had magic—*aura*—of its own.

My bare feet slapped against the tepid tiles as I made my way to the counter, my attention drawn to the stack of plush towels sitting in front of me. I eagerly grabbed one from the top, letting the soft fibers caress my face as I pressed it against my skin.

I caught a glimpse of my reflection in the foggy mirror. Wrapping the towel around my body, I tucked the end into itself and used it to gently wring the moisture from my hair. A small stream of water dripped onto the floor, creating a puddle at my feet. I glanced around the counter in search of a brush of some kind—all these guys had such long hair, there had to be a brush around here.

I stare at my clouded reflection, raising my hand and swiping it across the mirror's moving surface. My hand immediately stuck to it, and I pulled my hand back, but the goo held tight to my skin. It pulled away from the mirror and snapped back, sending ripples throughout its surface. I wiggled my hand in

113

hopes of breaking up the strange liquid, but my hand sank deeper into the opaque, blue abyss. My small sliver of peace shattered.

I struggled, trying to pull my hand free, but with each movement, the liquid tightened its grip on me, pulling me further into the chilled, reflective surface.

Panic crept into my bones; my mind whirring as I realized what was happening. My hand was wrist deep into the mirror, and no matter how hard I tried, I couldn't pull it out.

"Uh, hey?" I called out.

"Hey!" I tried again, more desperate this time. My arm was now elbow deep, the counter biting into my hip.

I banged my other fist against the counter. *Slurp!* The jelly pulled me in further, and now my bicep was disappearing. My towel fell to the floor around my feet, but I didn't care. Of all the things I thought would kill me here, a mirror definitely wasn't on the list.

"Lucille? Heads up," called a voice through the door. A soft knock followed, then the sounds of the door whooshing open. "I'm coming in!"

The tiniest sense of relief filled me when I saw it was Seymour here to save me from the carnivorous mirror. Seymour's eyes widened as he entered the room. He scanned my naked body, his face paling at the sight of me. My cheeks flushed with embarrassment and anger.

With a few quick strides, he stationed himself behind me. I could feel his eyes on me, and my skin pebbled, feeling exposed and vulnerable. I had bigger things to worry about than my bare ass and everything else being on full display. I'd bottle this humiliating situation and put it right on the shelf next to the rest of the trauma. The fact I was being eaten alive by a goddamn jelly mirror was, unfortunately, taking precedence.

"I didn't expect…" he began. I could see his contorted reflection in the movement of the mirror, his eyes raking across my bare shoulder blades.

"Yeah, I'm naked. You're welcome for the free show. My *arm*!" I spat, but it came out more like a growl as I jerked my body back, knocking into his silken chest.

"I told you not to touch the mirror," Seymour mumbled, placing a hand between my shoulder blades and pressing me forward. I shifted, already feeling the bruises forming on my hips. My cheek was millimeters from the carnivorous surface, and my stray, damp strands of hair fell forwards. The tips clung to the jelly reflection.

A hissed whisper filled the air. *"Home… here nor there, your heart lay empty. Stripped of your birthright, burdens a plenty. The heart…you seek… frail yes, but not weak…"*

"What did you say?" I asked.

"Huh?" Seymour moved his arms around my bare torso and yanked me back. With a wet pop, my arm was freed. Even though I didn't feel the pain, I had expected it to be gnawed and mangled to the bone. I was glad to see my flesh was intact and oddly dry.

"Did it talk to you? The mirror, did it say something?" Seymour turned me around, one hand on my shoulder, the other on my cheek. His eyes were a sea of cerulean blue, a thin strip of gold actively swirling around the outermost part of his iris. I wasn't sure how I'd never noticed the peculiarities of his eyes, because they were awe-inspiring. Like the sun setting over a rich sea.

"I—I don't know. Yes? Something about an empty heart and birthrights," I started, raising my arms to cross them over my chest in an attempt to savor even a morsel of what was left of my dignity. "I thought that was something your freaky ass was whispering to me as you felt up my naked body."

Anger. My one and only mask.

I jerked from his grasp, the concern in his eyes making my stomach uneasy. He was my captor. He didn't *really* care. I couldn't forget that. I couldn't fall into his kindness. His hands fell to his sides, his emotions changing into something foreign as he scanned my face.

"Don't tell Bas," he warned.

"Don't tell *Bas* what? That you were feeling me up or that the mirror spoke?"

Seymour scoffed, rolling his eyes as he turned away, heading to the door. "You're lucky it was me who offered to come to your aid. Get dressed, will you? Or do you need help with that too?"

I chewed at the inside of my cheek, choking back sarcasm as if it were poison.

Where was that damned gown?

As if the gown had heard my thoughts, a glimmer flashed in the corner of my vision. I closed my eyes slowly, letting out a sigh.

Of course. Because why wouldn't it appear out of thin air?

Snatching the dress, I stuffed myself into it.
Unfortunately, it was the most luxurious feeling fabric I'd ever felt.
It was hard to find things to despise when everything felt like pure
luxury.

The dress was extremely light on the body, the fabric so
silky it felt almost like a breeze against my skin. I turned back to
the devilish mirror; the reflection had calmed back to a smooth
surface. The dress kissed my curves perfectly, the low-cut front
was modest enough to prevent anything from slipping out but sewn
in a way that it displayed my chest well. The back, on the other
hand, was fully open and pulled right below the curvature of my
spine.

I snorted, rolling my eyes as I imagined this was what a
dress woven from spider webs would feel like—which it probably
was. It was probably some weird mystical spider whose sole
purpose was configuring gowns. I barked a laugh.

Well, I could be wearing worse things.

I looked at my soiled pile of tattered clothes,
remembering I had slipped my cell phone into my pocket back in
the library.

My phone!

I didn't know what I would do with it. I didn't have
anyone to call for help. 911? That seemed irrational—what were
they going to do? Would cell service even work between realms?

My feet slapped across the toasted floor, my hands
searching throughout the rank pile of clothes. My heart nearly
sprang through my chest and started river dancing when my fingers
touched the hard plastic.

Yes!

I pawed at the screen, disappointed but not surprised it was absolutely smashed. It wouldn't even turn on.

Unbelievable.

Frustration ravaged my brain, and I slammed the phone face down onto the tile. I wanted to scream at the foolish morsel of hope I had just felt.

"Waiting on you!" Seymour called.

With a huff, I stood and stomped my way out of the bathroom, slamming the door behind me. Cyx lounged casually on the chaise, and Seymour stood beside him. It was bizarre seeing Cyx in such a relaxed position, though I could still feel his eyes on me, scouring every inch of my body. I could feel the heat rising in my cheeks as I tried to ignore him and focus on Seymour. His gaze was so heavy on me, piercing me as if they had sprouted legs and began a march over every inch of my body. I straightened under his stare, my body betraying me as I posed ever so slightly, pulling my shoulders back.

Seymour clicked his tongue.

"Here I am." I flailed my arms in annoyance. "Happy now?"

"So snippy, human," Seymour started with a curl of his lips. I rolled my eyes and let out an exasperated sigh. I was in no mood for his smart remarks.

"Lucille," I growled, voice just above a whisper. "It's Lucille." I was so tired of being called demeaning things like *filth, soiling, human.* The least they could do was use my name when speaking to me.

Seymour's eyes softened, the lines beside his eyes relaxing.

"Yes, Lucille. I am happy, thank you for asking." He clapped a hand on Cyx's shoulder, jostling him side to side. "I've arranged a little something for you, since you've been such a good…guest? Ab…ductee?" He laughed at his own words. It seemed like whatever emotion had stirred in him in the bathing room had dissipated.

"No." I folded my arms across my chest.

Seymour blinked.

"But I didn't even say what it is?"

I curled my lip, snarling, "Don't care. Don't want to hear it. Don't *want* it, unless this is you guys deciding to free me."

"Well, it's kind of freeing. You'll get to go outside—kind of. I—you know it's not my place to make decisions on freeing you. But, even if it were, we can't." Seymour blushed.

I cackled. "Kind of freeing? I get to go outside *kind of.* Like a dog? It could be your decision to free me if you weren't so afraid of your Prince."

Seymour winced. I knew that last part struck right where I wanted it.

I caught Cyx bringing a hand up to his lips, covering a ghost of a smile.

Seymour's eyes rolled so far back; it was a surprise they didn't fall down his throat. "Original above! You're a prickly, tiny thing. I'm trying to do something nice for you, so this isn't wholly the worst experience. Bas is still out. He wants to keep you in this room, in the dark, until our next move in this…journey. But, well."

He tossed his hair side to side, wisps of moonlight locks floating around his face with grace. "I don't see him around here, so being his self-proclaimed second in charge means *I have a say in this small matter*. I say you can go out! Everyone should have the chance to see Amisa at least once in their lives! Now, I'm not saying you can—or should—walk the street, or slide into any of the clubs, or dance taverns for that matter, but… at the least I feel like I—we owe it to you." There was a flash of sadness that sprinted through his eyes.

I stood there, letting his words run in one ear and out the other. Though I could never let it show, I appreciated his kindness. On the other hand, all I heard was a chance for me to make a break for it. Was this guy really dense enough to think I would go down without a fight? Sure, I didn't know anything about the Magic Realm—or any other realm, for that matter—but I knew I was a fighter, and the least I could do was make this as much of a challenge for them as I could.

"Fine," I said curtly.

"Excellent! Not that I was *actually* giving you this option." He beamed, winking at me. If he winked at me one more time, I would pluck those little blue marbles right out of his skull.

"Cyx will be your escort on this fine evening." Seymour slammed a hand onto Cyx's shoulder. I still refused to look in his direction. Seymour slid his hand down to Cyx's chest and slapped his hand against the front of his shirt. Cyx shifted so slightly away from Seymour that he hadn't noticed, but I did. "You see, hu—Lucille, if Bas returns early, he'd never dare to throw hands with Cyx here."

Did Seymour make him uncomfortable?

My words were heavy with venom, "And he'd carve the floor with you just like he did before, huh?" I winked back at him. What a slippery little snake, throwing me a bone and throwing his friend under the bus in the same move. I gotta admit, I applaud that.

Seymour jaw cocked to the side, his eyebrows shooting up to his hairline.

"Yeah, okay, fine. Whatever." I raised my hands, feigning defeat, then dropped them, letting my hands smack against my thighs.

Cyx rose from the lounge chair, Seymour's hand sliding from his body. With four long strides, he was standing beside me, his eyes forward and elbow pointed toward me. Seymour and Cyx locked eyes and gave each other a subtle nod they probably thought I wouldn't notice.

"Well," Seymour said, his voice slightly serious. He gestured to Cyx. "I'll leave our guest in your capable hands. I've got *things* that need my attention." With a bow of his head, he turned and stalked out of the room to the bathroom.

Left standing there with Cyx, I could feel his eyes on me as I hesitantly turned my face up to him, flashing him a full smile. His expression was unreadable.

"So," I said awkwardly, breaking the thick wall of silence surrounding us.

"Lucille." His voice was warm like hot honey. His arm was still extended out to me.

I cautiously slid my arm through Cyx's. It was like

121

linking arms with a giant, and I'd never felt so fragile and powerless in my life. A seed of fear sprouted in my stomach as I thought of Sebastien catching me out of the room. It was pretty clear they were breaking some type of rule. I raised an eyebrow at him skeptically.

"And your boss will be fine with this? If he returns and we're still—"

"Prince," Cyx breathed huskily. With that one word, I suddenly wondered what my name would sound like if it were to drip from his lips in that husky tone.

"Thirty minutes until dawn breaks," Cyx warned. He walked us to the door that neighbored the bathroom, and I nodded. I wasn't sure if he was speaking to me, himself, or to Seymour in the other room. I didn't like that tone.

"Seymour?" Cyx called out.

Seymour replied with something inaudible from the bathroom before popping his head out of the door again and waving us off, a smile plastered on his face.

"Oh, go. Go!"

Cyx bent his arm in, resting his forearm against his torso. My hand felt so small and meek on his arm. When we reached the door, I could sense the hesitation in Cyx as he reached for the handle. He was tense. Was he wary about this? As he opened the door, I immediately scanned the halls—not only for a potential escape route, but for Sebastien.

Nothing.

My nerves relaxed a hair, seeing no sign of that bratty prince. There were no other doors for rooms, just a brass elevator parallel to our room, which was big, but not big enough for the whole floor to be ours.

CHAPTER 14
CYX

Seymour's audacity never ceased to amaze me. Of the centuries of knowing him, he had always stayed true to himself. A sneaky, conniving, self-centered little prick. It took effort to be unchanging.

I remembered when I first joined the Hellebore family's guard—starting as Bas' personal guard, then entering the war ranks. A refugee seeking solace in their territory, I caught the eye of the king during royal guard trials. The queen had always despised that. Despised me. I spent decades watching her talons dig deep into that shifter's skull—even the king's, as she seethed at my presence.

The girl pulled away from me slightly, her neck craning as she looked down the endless hallways. I didn't know what she expected to find, but I doubted she was stupid enough to run. I pulled her with me into the golden elevator. Her anxiety rolled off her, but I couldn't tell whether it was fear of me, of Bas finding out about this, or of the situation as a whole.

She was different. There was something not quite soilborn about her. She had a light that wasn't exactly same aura as the folk of this realm, but it felt…adjacent. I knew Bas had also noticed something off about her the moment he'd examined her in Ehn. And Seymour? That little snake had made it as clear as the three suns with the way he clamored after her.

My teeth ground together as I stifled my irritation. The way he talked to her as if she were an old friend. It made my blood boil. But there was something about her that called to me.

I pressed the glass button that read "RG1" and relinquished my thoughts to the soft hum of the elevator filling my ears.

CHAPTER 15
LUCILLE

Cyx's body radiated heat within the golden walls of the elevator. Our fuzzy reflections shimmered around us. I didn't understand Seymour's kindness; this gesture of simulated freedom didn't sit right with me, and while I didn't trust him wholly, something told me I could trust his kindness.

The doors slid open in a quiet, pressurized *whoosh*. We were on what appeared to be a rooftop, but the grove of trees rising from plots of glittering soil in the vast space before us made this space so congested, it was hard to tell whether this was a roof at all. The sprawling greenery opened its arms wide for us as Cyx walked us forward, leaving the cemented platform and onto squishy, emerald ground. Once my eyes adjusted to the dimly lit scene around us, it was like stepping into a painting.

Obscure flashes of glitter twirled in clusters in the air. I squinted, realizing the flashes were tiny glowing bugs dancing around one another in small clouds of self-produced light. The bright, airborne piles glided around low hanging tree branches, swooping down in mini tornadoes around flowers, then shooting to the next low branch in hurried dances. Impulsively, I drew in my arm, pulling Cyx closer to me. The more I stared, the more the space revealed itself to me. The different species of plants were breathtaking—almost overwhelming.

"You brought me to a garden?"

"Botanical garden," he corrected.

My mind couldn't keep up with my eyes. There was too much to see, too much beauty. My heart fluttered as I took a step further toward the sea of foliage. The ground was riddled with thick patches of spongy moss that felt plush and bouncy beneath my bare feet. I walked to a sprawl of flowers before me. They glowed with various gossamer-like iridescent petals that shined like solidified Aura Borealis lights. The tiny glowing bugs danced in and out of the trumpets, their little flickering bodies giving the illusion of sparkles.

I continued down the lush, mossy path that ran alongside more bundles of obscure flowers. As I got closer, I realized they were much bigger than I originally thought. Each head was the size of a dinner plate with petals that curled into spiral cones and tiny trios of trumpets nestled deep within the centers. I brought a hand up to touch the iridescent petal, and the warm caress of my finger left a bioluminescent blue streak that contrasted the rainbow of color, before disappearing almost as quickly as it was made.

"This is…breathtaking," I whispered to myself in disbelief.

"It is," Cyx replied, his voice close.

I looked up to find him a step away, the intensity in his eyes causing my heart to leap into my throat. I couldn't decipher the emotions behind them as the corner of his mouth curled upwards ever so slightly.

"Go on, you can explore. There's nowhere you can go where I won't find you," Cyx said, his voice so soft the words felt like warm honey slipping over my skin.

"Seymour told me you're a Portal Mage? So…" I stepped toward a collection of pink flowers whose stamen shone bright under the moonlight. I brushed my fingertips along the pink petals, unable to stop my curiosity. The petals curled in on themselves, encapsulating the stamen. "Like a wizard?"

Cyx huffed a laugh. "Not necessarily."

My head whipped toward the foreign sound, and I couldn't stop myself from grinning even if I'd tried.

"Yeah, you don't look like a wizard. No long gray beard or wrinkly skin." Did I just say that? I must have, because his eyebrows shot up as I continued rambling. "How old are you anyway? Or I guess, all of you?"

His return to silence made me want to bury myself into the moss under my feet. I turned to the pink flower whose petals were already beginning to unfurl.

"Around three hundred and sixteen years, give or take. Still young," he said as if he were still calculating.

I didn't know what I was expecting to hear, but as outlandish as that age was, it checked out—because why wouldn't the Faery, Shapeshifter, and Mage be anything less than three hundred years old?

His footsteps drew close. "And you?"

I looked at him, feeling foolishly childish. "Twenty-eight."

Something in his eyes shifted, as if his walls were coming down, brick by brick, for during this moment alone. I pulled my arms in, cradling them against my chest, rubbing the spot where our bodies had touched.

He had taken me to the garden. Not just a garden, but the most astonishing one I'd ever seen. Not only that, but he was talking casually with me. Things almost felt normal for the first time since I was brought here. Something about that had replaced the ravenous moths within my stomach with light butterflies. Wholeheartedly, allowing myself this moment, I smiled at him.

His face twisted into a smile that seemed to match mine, but maybe I was reading too into it.

"What?" he asked.

"Nothing. Well, I don't know. I didn't think you could smile? Or laugh, I guess?" I lowered my eyes to the ground, my toes squishing into the spongy floor as if it were the first time I'd ever noticed my own feet before.

"I smile," he stated with a flat voice, as if something in him had deflated. The tone unexpectedly stung my heart. I could tell by the sound of his leathers whining that he was shrugging. I lifted my eyes to him, eyeing the daggers lining his arms as they caught in the moonlight.

"Do they bother you?" he asked.

My face twisted into a scowl. "Who? Seymour and Sebastien? Seymour's fine, a little strange, but he's honestly been pretty nice. Your boss, though, he can get f—"

Cyx laughed. He *laughed*. Not a chuckle, but a warm, hearty, soulful laugh. It sounded so *normal*. A roar of goosebumps spread across my skin at the rich, molten sound.

"What's so funny? You asked if they bothered me." My cheeks were on fire, but his moss laced oak eyes danced.

"The weapons. I was asking if they bother you. Whether they make you uncomfortable. I was intending to conceal them better if they had, but I am reassured of your feelings for my comrade and the prince." His fingers swiped at his eyes.

Something in my heart hardened suddenly, as if an iron door had slammed shut. "Why does my comfort matter? What do you care?" I quipped, reverting my gaze to the galley of flowers. Feigning interest in an obscure bunch of cone-like fuchsias, I tilted my head up to the sky, filling my lungs with the earthy, warm air. Three bright white crescents smiled down at me.

CHAPTER 16
CYX

She was drenched in a cascade of moonlight that seemed to flow around her in cold soft waves. The light flowed around me. Through me—reaching into the depths of my being. The warm city air floated through the fibers of her dress, small sparkles shining like diamonds as they caught in the light. She was so angry, so volatile. It made sense, of course. I would be too, if I were in her situation. I could only imagine that her confusion and anger toward us was just the tip of the iceberg.

My heart clenched, *déjà vu* spearing through it like an arrow. Fragmented memories fluttered through my mind. I could feel something was off about her. It had been gnawing at me this entire time as I tried to figure it out.

I looked at the human in front of me, her brows furrowed in thought as her hair whipped in the breeze, a barely detectable glow emanating from her skin.

Unknowingly, she wove her soul seamlessly into mine.

And this wasn't the first time.

CHAPTER 17
LUCILLE

I turned toward Cyx, whose eyes bore into me with such intensity, it nearly sucked the air from my lungs. I averted my gaze immediately.

"I really miss the world making sense," I mumbled, squeezing my eyes shut in hopes that when I opened them, I'd be back home.

"The worlds have never made sense. Most simply fail to see that." He brushed a finger alongside my shoulder blades, letting his fingers slip through my hair before sliding my waves all the way to one side. My breath caught in my throat, a squeal emerging from the depths of my lungs on the brink of escape. Cyx was right beside me. I hadn't even heard him move. I gave a half-hearted laugh, angling my body slightly so his hand fell over my skin.

"First a smile, then almost a conversation. I didn't think you were allowed to show emotions, let alone talk outside of commands," I bit.

His eyes widened a fraction but stopped in place, unwavering. He regarded me as he lifted a hand up to my face, reaching for me as if he planned to caress my cheek. "I didn't think I'd ever see you again, yet here we are, little dove."

I jerked my head back. "Excuse me?"

What the hell did he just say?

His hand dropped, his head snapping to the side, and he went rigid. The walls that had fallen briefly before now stood more erect than ever.

"The prince is back. We need to get back to the room." He offered me his elbow again. When I didn't respond, he snatched my hand, tucking it between his forearm and torso. "Now."

I tried to yank my arm free, but it was trapped, and he was already on the move toward the elevator. "You're seriously going to pretend you didn't just say that?"

His eyes remained forward as I searched them for a morsel of the emotion that was there just moments ago.

"I don't know what you're talking about," he said, as if he didn't just tell me he thought he'd never see me again. What does that even mean!

I looked over my shoulder at the green oasis at my back, sadness forming in me as I realized I would likely never see this garden again.

"But we just got here," I murmured, the whine in my voice making me want to rip my own teeth out.

Pulling me into the elevator after him, we were back in the golden cage.

When we exited the elevator, voices vibrated through the walls. Opening the door for me, Cyx extended a hand and beckoned me into the viper pit.

"Look who's returned! Our filthy human, all clean and no longer smelling like the underbelly of hell." Sebastien's words slammed into me like a thrown stone. I bit down on the inside of my cheek; blood coated the side of my tongue as he continued.

"So glad you both are back from your little play date," he drawled. Every word that left his mouth was laced with pure venom. His green eyes soured as he looked between Cyx and me.

"Must you always yell? Original above, Bas!" Seymour slid out of the bathroom door, the hatch clicking softly behind him.

Bringing my hands to my face, I pressed my palms into my eyes. I felt like I was just existing here and watching myself from a bird's-eye view. Every moment in these places gave me whiplash.

Sebastien began to walk, prowling as though he were a lion circling his prey while I felt exposed and raw. The moments from the garden seemed like a mere dream now I was back in his presence. I still didn't understand why he hated me so much or how this place could even exist, how it was possible that magic, Faeries, and shapeshifting white-haired men were even a thing. What had Cyx meant? Why was I even here? What was the purpose of this?

"This will do," Sebastien snarled, his words like curdled milk.

Maybe there was a high price for girls here…Human girls. Maybe the people—the *things* here—viewed humans as some exotic oddity. I was about to vomit.

Sebastien stalked closer, his prowling circle getting

tighter and tighter with each pass. The fabric hugging my body felt suffocating as his eyes devoured me.

Sebastien stopped behind me where the back of the dress hung open, the fabric resting just above my tailbone. The sudden heat of his fingertips on my skin sent my heart to my throat. He slid his fingers through my hair, tossing a length of it in front of me. I could feel his eyes on my exposed skin, so I threw my hair back to cover the bareness. Sebastien huffed, humming in what sounded like an approval.

I stepped backwards to the door, resting my hand on the cool, ornate handle.

"No, no, no, rat," cooed Sebastien.

"You're painfully easy to read, you know that right? So daft. Do you sincerely believe you can escape?" Sebastien clicked his tongue and paused, his head tilting with a thought. He grabbed my shoulder, roughly guiding me next to Seymour.

My tongue felt numb and heavy in my mouth. That granule of happiness I had felt in the garden was now washed away with the acrid essence of Sebastien.

I watched as he prowled around the room, collecting things and shoving them into his pockets. He was adorned head to toe in a river of black silk. His unkempt hair was tied at the top of his head in a messy bun, revealing his pointed ears. Something about the sight of his ears tickled me, making me want to laugh. They looked absolutely ridiculous.

He caught my stare, cocking a thick eyebrow up as he dragged his eyes from mine down to my muddy toes that peeked out from under the gown, then slithered then right back up to my face. He was insufferable, and the arrogance that seeped from his pores was damn near tangible.

"Pissy elf," I whispered to myself, peeling my eyes away and picking at invisible dirt beneath my fingernails.

Beside me, Seymour stifled a laugh, the sound catching in his throat. The edge of my mouth pulled into a smirk.

"Come again?" Sebastien bit out. I didn't bother to look at him, choosing to ignore him instead. I already knew from his tone, his face was contorted with annoyance.

I stole a glance at Seymour, lines crinkled beside his sapphire pools. His head bobbed in a subtle nod as if to say, *good one*.

How could they bear to serve this man? Prince or not, there was no way they could stand Sebastien. I understood loyalty, but seriously?

There was a flash of something in Sebastien's eye, and something hard smacked me in the forehead. I brushed my face, gritty taupe flakes raining down my vision. A crusty roll laid beside my feet. I kicked it back toward the prince.

"Not hungry."

His cheeks flared, but it was true. To my surprise, I wasn't hungry. I actually felt totally fine. My body no longer ached, and I wasn't nauseated with dehydration. I honestly couldn't remember a time I had felt this good, this solid.

His jaw cocked to the side, and I shrugged him off.

"Don't worry, he likely found it in the trash," Seymour snickered beside me.

Sebastien snatched the roll from the floor, his fingers

bright with electricity. I didn't pretend to understand how magic worked. I felt like I was past that at this point, and I just accepted his little tantrum show of sparks as the bread in his palm disintegrated.

His emotions were easy to read; he was a man who waved his emotions around like a flag. I knew he wanted me to fear him, and I knew it pissed him off that I didn't, so I scoffed.

Sebastien's viridescent eyes burned into mine.

"We will be on foot through Amisa until we reach the gateway. You will not speak, look, react, or wander. You will not touch or consume anything anyone gives you. You will not so much as inhale in the direction of anything or anyone." Sebastien stalked closer to me with each word. "Do you understand that, you insufferable soilborn rat?"

He stopped in front of me, standing so close I could smell him, the air full of honey and cedar.

"You will not—"

"Oh my god, do you like to hear yourself talk that much? You want me to exist solely like some puppet. I got it the first time. Don't touch stuff, don't drink stuff, don't look at stuff. Don't, don't, *don't.* Anything else? Or are you done?" I burst. These nagging commands were nails, and my soul was a chalkboard. A flame ignited within me, mirroring the fire in his eyes. His fist clenched and unclenched, his veins glowing beneath midnight silk. My breath grew shallow and slowed.

"You cannot speak to the prince this way!" Cyx stepped into my line of sight, his low voice reverberating through me. I squeezed my eyes shut.

Seymour laughed, clapping his hands as if we were performers putting on a show for his sole entertainment. My hands balled into fists, my fingernails biting into my flesh.

"Your back will remain covered." Sebastien continued as if I hadn't spoken at all. "Do you understand me, rat?"

I screamed. The sound that escaped me was borderline unearthly, and I could have sworn the floor shook beneath me.

I screamed until there was no air left in my lungs and my throat felt raw, and no sound was left in me. The silence that followed was loud. Only then did I open my eyes.

"Lucille," I said, my voice breaking. "It's Lucille. *My name.* I am so sick of being treated as less than a living being." I breathed deep as the three men stared at me with wide eyes.

Their stunned silence gave me strength.

"Not rat. Not soilling. Not human. Not vermin." I closed in on Sebastien. "You command me around and bark at me as if I had a choice in any of this. Do you think I want to be here? Why am I even here? What do you want from me? Do you think being a prince means anything to me? It means *nothing* to me. You are nothing more than a convoluted, insufferable, arrogant prick."

Sebastien's nostrils flared. His hand shot up, grabbing my face. His pointer finger and thumb dug into my cheeks, pressing the flesh painfully into my teeth. I heard his magic before I felt it, that same burning feeling from before.

"Do it," I eked out. Sebastien clamped his fingers harder, the meaty flesh of my inner cheeks stinging as my teeth sawed against them, iron coating my tongue.

"I can't stand you," he growled, molten light stinging my

lips, forcing them shut.

Then kill me.

As if reading my thoughts, he gripped tighter.

Two sets of hands clasped his shoulder

"Bas," Seymour said. The two men worked at pulling him away.

"Sir, the suns have fully…" Cyx coaxed.

With a huff, he released my face and brashly tossed me to the side. The light sealing my lips dissipated with the movement. Tears stung my eyes, but I forced them down.

"Cut through the clubs. No streets, no marketplaces, no mingling. Weave through the clubs and alleys until you reach the edge of the city." Sebastien scanned his two companions. "Will you have enough aura for the next jump, Cyx?"

Cyx nodded stiffly. I looked at him, allowing my eyes to trace over his features for a moment. It was as if his every feature held a role in his perfection. I studied the way his hair cascaded over his shoulders in molten dark waves when Cyx's eyes met mine.

There was something bizarrely familiar about him, something that felt safe. *Crap, was this how Stockholm Syndrome began?* The ghost of a smile washed over his mouth, and I looked past him before and gazed up toward the ceiling, hoping to give the illusion I was checking out the room and not him as heat flooded me.

Sebastien began another onslaught of commands once more, repeating all the same things he'd already said, making sure the instructions were carved into the folds of our brains. The way he kept repeating himself and over-explaining told me he was nervous about something, and the unknown soured and chewed away at the lining of my stomach.

Seymour slid next to me.

"We got the plan, Bas. Protect our Lucille. We go through; we get out. Kill whatever gets in our way. Meet at the gateway." Seymour's words were smooth, but there was a slight bit of annoyance behind them, as if he were humoring his prince rather than taking heed.

"As if I'd let anything happen to this pretty Lucille." Seymour's hand brushed against the exposed skin of my back, his warm fingertips running along the top of my spine and across my shoulder blades.

Sebastien watched his every move, an unknown emotion reflected in his eyes as Seymour wrapped his arm around me and pulled me in tight. Looking down at me, he smiled. Sebastien stormed through us, making a point of forcing us apart with his charging body, then he slammed the door behind him.

CHAPTER 18
SEBASTIEN

As I exited the luxurious grasp of the hotel on my own, the sounds and sights of the bustling Amisaan streets immediately engulfed me. She set such a fire in my veins. How could something so beautiful be so infuriating? Her very essence crawled beneath my skin with every word and glance. She made me irate! She could smile and laugh with Seymour. Hell, Cyx even took her to the garden! He had very seldom ever defied my command. I assumed when he returned from patrol he would be a second set of eyes on the girl, but the next thing I knew, I returned to him on the roof with her. I'd *have* to reprimand him for that later.

The image of Seymour touching Lucille's back replayed in my mind. My jaw cracked from tension. Why was Seymour hovering around her so much? Constantly smiling at her, laughing. Did he think I hadn't caught every wink he'd thrown her way? He didn't even like women, let alone humans! And the light in her eyes when she smiled at him, even the way she'd stolen looks at Cyx when he wasn't looking at her.

Yet, when she looked at me—a Fae prince—it was as though she wanted to skin me and roll me in acid. We Fae were among the most beautiful beings in this realm, and she looked at me as if I were a pile of excrement!

I grimaced, jealousy bittering my mouth. I had secretly

held onto an echo of a wish to see her reaction when she saw the Amisaan flowers at night because she was just so expressive. One could read the emotions on her face like a book.

But it was my duty to bring her to Mother, and I couldn't allow myself to let these budding emotions bloom. At least I knew my comrades' fondness for her would encourage them to be hyper aware of their surroundings today. I had no doubt they would gut anything or anyone that showed the slightest threat or interest in her.

I shook my head, hoping to clear my mind. This whole venture was a high-stakes gamble, and a small part of me was beginning to fret that I may not be able to pull this off. It was a struggle every second to be so cruel to her.

Mahni, the leader, the *king* of this district, had always been one for grandeur and ostentation, with a hint of showmanship. He was well known as the trickster among the Royal Fae. He often used his swell of aura for illusion to indulge in hedonistic pleasures rather than for practical purposes. His opulent city was hidden deep under the shifting sands of Amisa, like a trapdoor spider's intricate nest. The cluttered streets swarmed with a diverse mix of Fae, Shifters, and obscure creatures from all corners of Nyria, moving in intoxicating patterns.

I took a deep breath, inhaling the warm desert air into my lungs. The section of town we were in was lined with towering buildings illuminated by pulsing neon lights that seemed to beckon and seduce passersby. Drunken giggles and slurred conversations whirled around me, the skin around their snouts and mouths dusted with a particular bioluminescent substance—no doubt high on

Siren Scale, which seemed to be the drug of choice here despite the realm-wide ban. Royalty would do as royalty pleased, regardless of the near extinction of an entire kind.

Stepping back, I placed the heel of my boot against the marbled wall of the hotel, leaning my head against the sturdy surface, savoring the coolness that pressed past my hair and to my scalp. The saving grace of this city of bingers was how easy it was to become another face in the crowd. Everyone was trying to drown their sorrows one way or another, rarely paying attention to anyone else around them.

The door beside me swung open and Cyx stepped out, Seymour on his heels with Lucille still tucked under his arm, pinning her hair against her bare skin. I watched as he leaned down and crooned something in her ear, making her solemn face blossom into a small smile. For a moment, her calculating eyes were calm as if she was trying to formulate an escape, though it would be less than wise of her. Where did she think she could run off to?

Humans, always fighting. Always running. Their kind never stopped to think about all the possibilities at hand—only what was directly in front of them. It was no surprise their garbage heap of a realm had been imploding for ages. I'd always wondered when we'd witness the Ethereal washing itself of that leech of a realm.

I let the three of them take the lead. Seymour on the left, Lucille in middle, Cyx on the right, and me a few paces behind, my eyes fixated on her back. Her head swiveled and bobbed as she took in her surroundings.

Mahni's glamor gave the perfect illusion of being under the skies, from the warm breeze that circulated the streets to the glittering triple mooned sky of Nyria. It was devastating, precise, and irritatingly clear the Amisaan king had spared no time with perfecting and fine-tuning his craft of illusions.

I saw Lucille's side profile over her shoulder, her mouth agape with wonder and awe as I followed the line from her eyes to the sky. The simulated desert sky held both night and day in an immaculate illusion of both. It could drive one mad if they didn't know it was an illusion.

Nonetheless, the sight of her enthralled by this measly use of aura sent pin pricks in my chest. I did, however, savor this sight for a moment. Her profile looked as though the Original above themselves had decided to pour every ounce of them self into forming her. The soft glow of the neon lights cast an enchanting glow around her in showers of pink and yellow. Between her perfect skin and jawline, the sparkle and innocence in her eyes was nothing short of angelic. My heart fluttered, the feeling leaving me with a sensation I hadn't felt in over three centuries.

She was awe-inspiring.

I reached my hand up just to rub the spot on my chest above my heart, hoping the action would dissolve the feeling. There was no reason to feel this way. She was not a marketplace pet, she was not a companion, and she should *not* be igniting such flames within me. I refused to allow myself to feel anything for her.

But still, the sensation was deep within my chest, crawling its way deeper and deeper until it nuzzled against my heart. I could not have feelings for this insignificant amalgamation of flesh and bone.

She was nothing more than a living safe. Her heart was the only thing that held any morsel of purpose, and she was only a vessel. I repeated the mediocre mantra in my head with each step.

Seymour turned his head ever so slightly, giving me a subtle nod.

My cue.

I watched them for a beat as they continued onward, Cyx parting the sea of beings and folk with just a glance at his sheer size. I slowed until I lost sight of them and turned into the first neon lit alleyway where characters lined the stone walls. I slipped through the door of a club nestled between a crude bioluminescent painting of a siren with over inflated assets and was immediately greeted by the sound of bass that was so strong, it was physical. The vibrations drowned out the electronic composition, running through my veins with an electrifying steady *thump, thump, thump-thump.* The smell of sweat was heavy in the air.

I navigated to a secluded high table. The perfect spot where I could see without being seen. The pulsing energy of this place filled me up, the sensation seducing me into temptation easily enough. It had been decades since I'd had a good drink—a server appeared at my table right on cue. I couldn't help but smirk and gave a silent nod to Mahni and his ways.

The server's skin shimmered like diamonds under the scorchflies' light while the neon lights bounced off part of her metallic scalp, sending a show of rainbows over her face.

I'd always been curious about those ones.

145

Her hair sprouted from her chrome flesh, a harsh pink swath that had been slicked back into an orderly ponytail, showing off her adorned pointed ears. Back when I had wanted to be a historian, these Cy-Fae had always fascinated me. I never understood how they came to be or even worked…or lived?

The creature's attributes were Fae-ish, but the insides were a web of wires and circuits. I'd never seen it for myself, but I could believe it, because when she turned, her black pearled eyes seemed to see right through me. Surely, there had to be a historian with a book somewhere that laid out the creatures' inner workings. I made a mental note to hunt that down when this is all over, as a nice reward of sorts.

Her blinks were robotic, each flutter of her pink lashes coinciding with a twitch of her head.

She leaned forward and pushed her breasts against the table, causing them to nearly spill over her too-tight top. It took every ounce of effort to avoid cringing—not the Cy-Fae's actions, at the reason behind it. I knew she was just playing her part in the club, but I couldn't help the ringing feeling of disgust.

"What can I get for you tonight?" she purred, her voice a low, metallic, seductive thrum. She leaned in further.

"Get those external lungs off my table, you sex bot," I growled, shooing her away with a flick of my wrist as if she were a pestering insect. "Fae-kiss. Dry."

Emotionless, she straightened and turned, disappearing into the swell of bodies. The club was nearly pitch black save for iridescent bubble-like orbs of encapsulated scorchflies—which were just enlarged glow bugs—and the occasional burst of neon laser that ran through the air in time with the music.

I watched the scorchflies, their blackened wings fluttering within their prison, pushing the bubble around the space, illuminating random sections as they passed aimlessly. Just past them, in the cages hanging from the vaulted ceilings, were dancing lylans whose wings had been mostly removed. Nonetheless, their movements were lithe and erotic, the candescent light from the scorchflies reflecting on their bare, glittering bodies. The cheers of the patrons made their snake-like smiles spread.

I had missed my realm, but I couldn't quite say I had missed Amisa. I turned my face into my hands, rubbing my forehead. The intoxicating beat seeped into me like a drug that made my head heavy and my throat thirsty. Propping my chin on my fist, I stared at the dance floor, watching the chaos of all forms of sweaty, glowing bodies gyrating against one another. There were Fae, faun-like beings with the haunches of a deer and torso of a man, the slick, blue bodied naiads with bubbles of water attached to their gills, and so many more. Everyone danced to the dense pounding of the bass, faces covered in the obvious glow of Siren Scale.

The waitress returned with a thimble-sized shot of shimmering green liquid. She placed it in front of me, staring at me as she awaited approval. Shooing her away, she quickly moved on to the neighboring tables. I swirled the lavish liquid in its miniature, crystalline glass before I took a sip of the wormwood derived beverage, praying it would at least dull the edges of the feeling that begun to fester in my heart. But even as the alcohol burned its way down my throat, tickling my insides, the tense

147

feeling in my heart remained. I returned my focus to the dance floor, scouring through the sea of mind-altered bodies.

Just past the bar were two brutish men standing on either side of a door. *Ah, there he was.* I drank the remaining drops of the spirit, running my tongue along the edge of the glass before tossing it over my shoulder.

I left the table and began my trek across the expanse of the sweat-slicked dance floor. Weaving and shoving past bodies, stepping on the hooves and webbed feet of patrons, no one seemed to notice as they continued with their frenzied movement. Hands pawed at me as I pushed through, even as various beings tried tempting me to stay.

"Bas?" hollered a familiar voice over the waves of sounds and figures. "Sebastien!"

I kept my eyes forward; there was no reason to cast my aura out to locate the voice. There were far too many heartbeats to sift through here. Even so, I didn't care enough. There was not a single living thing in this territory I cared to see—save for Mahni. I ignored the incessant call of my name, the voice familiar enough to be an acquaintance, but not enough to stop me as I weaved through the crowd.

The men at the door already had their beady golden eyes locked on me, glaring down their broad, furred snouts, canines bared. They easily had several feet on me. Amisa's primary inhabitants were fauns and their higher, royal bloodline of manticore.

This territory, along with the skeleton of the Myrnen district, were the only two areas of Nyria that were led by non-Fae folk. Nyrian historians theorized that during the creation of the Magic Realm, the Ethereal began combining creatures—splicing them—out of boredom to see what would survive. It was generally assumed the manticore were Fae-lion hybrids.

I stared up at one of the lion-faced men, his orange mane spread around his head like rabid flames, the fur beneath his chin braided with little gold orbs lacing throughout the plait.

"I'm here to pay a visit." My words came out almost like a yell, hoping they could hear me over the music. I nodded toward the door. "Mahni?" The manticore flared its nostrils in a huff. A rush of hot, rancid air cascaded over me.

"*King Mahni* no longer communes with club patrons inside or outside of these walls." stated the beast to my left, folding his paws in front of him as he puffed out his chest.

"Tell him it's Sebastien Hellebore." The beast stared at me for a moment, and I could see the confusion flash in his dimwitted eyes as the puzzle pieces slowly clicked into place. I clenched my jaw, my patience growing thin with the thick-skulled cats. "The *Hellebore prince*."

The manticore looked at one another, and then the one on the right reached one thick paw out behind him, lightly rapping a pattern on the door with his claws. There was a small shuffling followed by the sound of items falling to the floor.

"What do you want!" A baritone voice roared from behind the door.

"It's the Hellebore prince. He is here, My King," the left manticore bellowed.

The door cracked open slightly from behind their puffed

bodies. A marble of a saffron colored eye peeked through the sliver. The door snapped shut, the sounds of locks whirring from the other side.

"Sebastien, my boy! My favorite northerner!" Mahni exclaimed as he swung the door just wide enough for a meaty paw to shoot through, beckoning me to enter. "Come, come! Sit, little princeling! I heard how you slayed your own father! *Tsk tsk,* very bold of you! I never would have thought you had the balls! Oh, to see the look on Thaddeus's face when his own heir turned on him, what a day! What a day!"

Entering the room, I was met with a thick wall of humidity and the stench of alcohol, the dampness causing my silks to cling to my skin. In the center was a single birdcage on a pedestal. It housed a scorchfly with murky black wings that beat against the bars in a desperate attempt to escape. Contrasting the modern club on the other side of the door, this room was beyond dismal, especially with its various empty glass bottles and shattered glass strewn across the floor. The only other furniture was a large desk nestled near the left wall with two chairs sitting on either side, both engraved with flourishes.

"Sit, boy! Quit the formalities!" Mahni placed his paws on my shoulders, guiding me. The ornate desk before us was covered in more empty vials slicked with a bioluminescent, filmy slime.

The king slammed a crystal bottle in front of me. I could smell the potent Fae-kiss emanating from it mixing with the stench of alcohol on his breath. "Here. This will put some hair on that chest of yours! Much more potent than what's served out on the floor. Come on, give it a swig!" Mahni flashed a toothy, canine-filled grin as he beckoned me to drink the opulent green contents sloshing within the vessel like an angry tide threatening to drown me.

When I didn't respond, the king's eyes glazed over. By the smell of Mahni, it was clear he had already enjoyed more than his fill of the spirit. "Original above! I haven't seen you since you were in your early one-hundreds, isn't that so?"

He slumped heavily into the chair opposite me, his engorged stomach distended and straining against his wrinkled and stained clothing. His mane was matted and tangled; the jewels woven throughout it catching on his hair-like insects trapped in a web. He was a bloated, debauched figure, barely able to move under the weight of his own excess.

So much had changed.

Although he had never been the warrior type, he hadn't been...this. Whatever this gluttonous, overstuffed, drunken slug was, it bordered on pitiful. He reached a paw out to me, gesturing once again for me to drink.

Begrudgingly, I humored him, attempting to subtly wipe the mouth of the bottle before pouring a modest amount into my mouth.

"Ahhh, good boy! Just like your dad." Mahni slammed his paw on the desk, sending the empty vials rolling to the floor, before they shattered. "Give her here!"

I passed the vessel across the wooden surface and watched as he took a long, messy drink, ignoring the droplets of green spilling onto his mane.

"Now, princeling, to what do I owe the pleasure? How's that mother of yours? I suppose you wouldn't know, since she cast you out and what not. I haven't seen her in my territory since, well, before she wiped out Myrnen? Blessed that she hasn't come here. But this! This is such a treat!" Mahni sighed, shaking his head.

"A banished Fae royal, back from the Human Realm! Callahan must be foaming at the mouth to get her hands on you. Tell me, what hoops did that ol'bag have you go through to come back, huh? Boy, you should see the shit she's been doing since you murdered your pop." The king took another long swig, swallowing his senses with the liquor. "You know she's got a bounty out for you, right? You and your little clan."

No, I did not know that.

"A bounty?" I asked. He was drunk—just drunk enough I might coax what I need from him. I stretched out for the bottle, and Mahni scooted it lazily toward me. I raised the liquid to my lips, feigning a drink.

Mahni nodded enthusiastically, the charms in his hair jingling. He reached beneath his desk and revealed a tattered scroll.

"Mhm, sent these out just shy of two-hours ago." A loud, putrid belch released from his lips.

I grabbed the paper, reading the headline.

DEAD OR ALIVE WITH ALL ASSETS: SEBASTIEN HELLEBORE, CYX ANDROMEDI, SEYMOUR SEIN.

Scrawled below was a hefty sum of coins.

Assets. Dead or alive. All of us? She knew I had the human heart. None of this made sense. What was the point of a bounty when I was bringing her the human? Was this not what she

152

had explicitly wanted from me? What was the fairness in this? Give her the heart of a human, and my name would get cleared. I would regain my place in the royal court of Hellebore. Would she not want this? She was the sole bearer of the throne now, but the Hellebore line could not continue without me.

I wanted to rip my hair out.

"This makes no sense," I said, raking a hand through my hair and grabbing a handful. "She knows Fae can only bear a child once. She gave my father no other children. She'll end the Hellebore line if someone kills me! Folly—this is just an illusion. A prank!"

That had to be why she hadn't executed me before, right?

"I'm not wanting to meddle in your family drama, but this is no folly. Thad was a good man, ran his territory well. Very modestly kept territory. Ah, well, before Callahan dug her talons into him anyway." He exhaled a rancid sigh. "What you did to him, I'm sure you had your reasons. I've got things in my past I'm not proud of too, we all got 'em. But I'm not going to pawn you off to her. I'd watch my back if I were you. That crone's got her nails deep in almost every territory except mine." Mahni slammed his fist down on the desk again.

I snatched the vessel, this time taking a real swig. A real *long* throat scorching drink. My thoughts were beyond frenzied. My intentions were to receive a reading from Mahni; I knew he didn't do them often, but I needed to coax out answers about…Well, selfishly, about that human girl, if I were to be honest. The conflict she brought to my heart was terrifying, and the marks on her back stupefied me. But now with knowledge of this

153

bounty on us…

Dead or alive.

Mahni wiped his paw against his face, his round saffron eyes bloodshot. "Now, what do I owe the pleasure, huh? Did I ask that already? I can't hide you here, so don't ask. I'm not going to tell my people to keep their mouths shut, either. We've kept off that broad's radar thus far, and I admit, I admire you, but not enough to risk my territory." There was an apology in those drunk eyes.

I took another long slug of the Fae-kiss. A buzz had settled in the back of my skull, quieting my worries for a moment, the feeling crawling down my spine and throughout my whole body. Mahni pulled another bottle from under his desk, the liquid inside a deep, almost dark red that flashed to green in the blink of an eye. I ran my hand along the top of my head, pressing the tussled strands down.

"Here, princeling—you need it." He held the bottle out to me, the contents swirling. I snatched it from the king's grasp, popping the cork and tilting the vessel against my lips. The syrupy liquid slowly moved its way to my mouth, its scent cloying and sweet with hints of berries and spice. The humidity in the air amplified the smell, making it almost overwhelming as I drank, assaulting my tongue with the rich, sickly sweet flavor of tart berries and something I couldn't quite pinpoint. The liquid left a fiery sensation in its wake, throwing me into a coughing fit.

Mahni leaned back in his chair with a satisfied grin. I let out a small laugh myself before setting the bottle down on the desk and leaning forward, my elbows resting on my knees, my pulse now in my ears. I shook my head to clear the sensation and sound. There was no way I was drunk from a few drinks of Fae-kiss.

"Forgive me, it's been a good while since I've had proper drinks," I said, straightening.

Another chuckle escaped the king's maw. "No need, a well-deserved tribute. As I said, the honor is mine."

A wave came over me. "What's this about my mo—the Hellebore queen—you were saying? You alluded earlier that she's been up to something, no?" My vision began to swim as I looked at the king whose eyes seemed to double.

"Are you alright, boy? I wouldn't have figured a century in the Human Realm would leave you to be such a lightweight!" Mahni's voice wafted around me like an echo as I tried to focus on him. A crooked smile spread across his face as he rapped his nails on the dark wood of the desk. The blood in my veins thickened, feeling as though my platelets had turned to lead.

"A…m-m…er" The sounds were dense and clumsy as they left my lips, my lungs suddenly struggling to pull in sufficient air.

The door beside us creaked open, and the two manticore from the club walked in, their heavy feet crunching over glass, popping the vials that littered the floor. I faintly felt their presence as they stood behind me, the hairs on the back of my neck fighting to raise themselves. I lolled my head to the side to see them.

"Jahkin. Rimiel," Mahni commanded.

I heard the scrape of his chair moving, sluggishly turning back to the king. I watched as he rose and planted his two meaty paws firmly on the desk. His face contorted into a twisted mask of pure malice, the air around him seeming to vibrate.

The two manticore behind me shifted, inching closer, the aura permeating from them almost tangible. I tried to focus on Mahni, but my vision was still blurry. It felt like I was moving in slow motion; my thoughts formed as though they were moving through tar. Forming a single thought felt impossible.

Something was very wrong—a few proper drinks wouldn't have made me feel like *this*, no matter how long it had been. A rough, calloused paw clamped down on the back of my neck, sharp claws digging into my flesh and leaving deep imprints as they wrapped around the front of my throat. I struggled for breath, feeling his grip tighten as my limbs seized.

The room began to ripple, the air undulating and the walls moving as though they could breathe. Slowly, like a snake shedding its skin, the glamor around the room fell. The drab, musty room shifted into an elegant office, the floor revealing itself to be sleek erydian stone. The empty, shattered vials littering the floor vanished. The bottles I had been drinking from reshaped into a stout, dismal jug with the crude outline of a lylan etched on its face.

Lylan's blood.

Mahni let out a rough laugh, his voice now a thick and rumbling echo. "Sorry 'bout this, princeling."

A surge of fury rushed through me. How could I be so stupid? An outright fool! I tried to move, my arms failing to raise, my aura sluggishly fighting the lylan blood that was mixing in my veins. Their blood, at high volumes, held neurotoxins that could easily cause paralysis at best, or at worst, comatose conditions.

Idiot. Come on!

My aura sputtered to life, my fingertips electrifying, fueled by pure rage. *If I could just get one*—but then something shattered against my head, and warmth leaked from my skull and dripped down the side of my face. The soft flutter of the scorchfly's wings ceased, the light blinking out as darkness flooded the room.

CHAPTER 19
SEBASTIEN

Water poured over my head like a cruel metronome. Icy spheres slipped between my shirt and the hard surface at my back. I didn't know how long I had been out. If I hadn't stubbornly closed my mind off to Seymour, I could have requested his aid. But no. Of course not. My arrogance had overruled my reason. I had known this journey would be dangerous, but I had foolishly thought it would be the human at risk. Not me—not to this degree.

My mind still swam from the blow as words rose from around me, taking form as small murmurs before blooming into indistinguishable shouts.

"Are you that naive? Do you really think *me* to be that naive?" The voice was cold and seething, detached from all reason—manic.

"Fae. Your kind is truly pitiful. You carve the wings out of your own kind, yet flaunt yourselves to be the most omnipotent beings in the realm. That arrogance makes me ill. Open your damned eyes!" Strong hands gripped my face, shaking me violently.

The jostling sent chills down my spine, stiff vertebrae cracking painfully. The burning sensation in my veins had dulled to a heavy ache; the effects of the lylan blood had to have dissipated by now. I hadn't had enough to render me completely immobile, but it still took all of my strength to pry my eyelids open—only to be met with Mahni's snarling face.

His enraged eyes burned into mine, only inches away. His slit pupils were fully dilated, allowing me to see my gaunt reflection. His lips curled back to reveal glistening canines and strands of saliva dangling from his jowls.

"Don't you dare try to play me for a fool, princeling. I know that blood's wearing off!" Mahni barked, his saliva dripping onto my thigh and seeping through the silk. Hot, putrid breath filled my nostrils. He leaned closer, and I could see the anger burning in his eyes like a rabid lion ready to pounce as the fog clouding my brain dissipated with each passing second.

"What. Are you. Talking about?" The words fell sluggishly from my mouth, heavy and thick as if coated with invisible cotton. I struggled to pull my head back, his grip on my face unrelenting.

I strained to raise my hands and push him away, only to find they had been bound behind me. For a moment, my mind slipped to Lucille. I had done the same thing to her. Bound her and rendered her helpless to the same, vitriol treatment.

"That hound of a mother of yours has been eradicating the entire realm! She has clawed her way from the north to all surrounding territories. All in the last century! And you, Nyria be damned, *you* just so happen to reappear as she nears the southern lands, a bounty atop your head in my territory—alone!" Thick claws unsheathed as he yelled, his voice shrill while the needle-like tips pierced into the soft flesh of my cheeks. "To what! Corner Amisa? A convenient ploy to which we will not succumb. We will *not* bow to the bitch! You must think yourself so clever. The territories, the folk of this realm—we are not meant to rule under one name, but to rule together as one!"

The king released my face. Cold air rushed against my cheeks where his grip had been, soothing the sharp pain where his nails had no doubt left marks. I tracked his movement, watching as he sunk onto all fours, his tail whipping around him. My teeth pressed together, refusing to allow myself to succumb to the self-loathing thoughts that began to swarm my mind.

He stood, sauntering to me. "A drawn-out game of cat and mouse, is that it? Send the lone heir out to the Human Realm, for what reason? Distraction? Cultivate pity and build upon the bones of others?" His voice cracked as he looked at me with eyes full of disdain.

I could hardly comprehend his words as his glamor fully cracked, the room shifting. Every surrounding surface and wall warped and changed with each of the king's breaths.

"I. Don't. Know. What. You're. Talking. About." I reined in my thoughts, giving the binds around my wrists a flex.

Rope. He chose rope?

Mahni's face was exasperated and exhausted. This version of him was a stark contrast of the one earlier. This version of him, gut deflated, mane more than well groomed, and sleek? He looked nothing short of magnificent as the jewels and trinkets glimmered throughout his braids.

I couldn't confess to my comrades that I had fallen for Mahni's illusions. I'd never hear the end of it.

I cleared the phlegmy remnants of lylan blood from my

throat, spitting them at my side as I flexed against the ropes, feeling the straining fibers.

Lifting my chin a tick, I did my best to keep my voice low and level as I spoke. "Let me educate you, cat. Do you want to know how the Hellebore king was murdered? Did you know that during the war against Myrnen, the queen opted to be there with her people? She was there, not to give strength to the battalion, but to give a *show,* you ignorant animal." The words tumbled out of my mouth as rage surged through me.

"Did you know she used nothing but a thorn? A fucking *thorn.* Imbued with our very own family's flower nectar. One measly passing embrace with my father, and she dropped it into his leathers. Did you know that all it took was for him to move just the right way on the field, and it pricked his skin with the poison?"

He scoffed. "Lies! Nothing but lies to aid your mother's genocide." His lips curled, a string of saliva hanging from his fangs.

"Read me." I smirked. "See for yourself."

His tail swished feverishly around him. The floor blackened beneath my feet…

Blood coated my trembling hands as screams erupted from all sides, piercing my ears like sharp daggers clawing their way into my skull. I spat the blood in my mouth, staining the dirt beneath me. There was not a single part of me that wasn't aching, bruised, or lacerated.

A voice shouted through the chaos, "King Thaddeus!"

A battle-worn man with frayed wings landed feet away

from me. He sprinted toward me, his bloodshot eyes fixated to my left.

He had to have news to report. Maybe this hellish war was finally ending.

My skull pounded, my brain aching so fiercely, it was a challenge to even see straight. I struggled to make sense of my surroundings, the air heavy with smoke and the sounds of death.

I could feel wetness slipping out of my ear, down my neck. I'd been pushing myself far past my limits. Forcing aura from the land to fuel me in this battle. It was wreaking havoc on my brain, but I'd been utterly depleted of my own reservoir for days...weeks. No Fae, not even royalty, could abuse their aura for so long without reaping mortifying consequences.

I'd fought this entire war on foot, refusing my mother's orders of using my wings, but my magic...I had sent currents through thousands of innocent bodies...Women, children, the elders—scorching them from within. Turning their organs to ash. Turning my own insides to ash with each lash of my magic.

I was dying, and I knew it. Maybe it was for the better if I were to die in this war. I didn't think I could live another day doing this, let alone another century.

Blood-curdling screams flew to my ears, but I knew better than to look. I knew those screams—they were the screams of my ravens. My warriors getting their wings mutilated and dug out by the Shifters opposing us.

"Cast him! Cast the prince!" Ironed hands wrapped around my wrist.

"What's going on?" I fell to my knees in the gruesome

mud as someone shouted an order overhead to the back quarter commander.

"Kyn! Head to the front ravens! Inform Cyx that we are ready to head into the Sein estate!"

The front ravens? We surely must have defeated the enemy army, right? But why were they headed to the Sein estate?

"Commander, Cyx is no longer at the front lines," Kyn yelled back through screams.

I glanced to my side where my father laid just feet away. His bloodshot eyes were morbidly glazed and hollow, and curdled blood coated the side of his mouth. There was something that jutted out from the neckline of his chain mail. Did he get hit with shrapnel?

"Wh-what?" I croaked. A ball formed in my throat. I tried to shift toward my father, but the binds of the casting locked me in place. The scream that erupted from me was unbecoming.

"For fuck's sake!" The man wound his fist into my blood crusted hair. My body was so feverishly wrought with exhaustion, I could feel my mind slipping into darkness.

My father was dead.

Darkness filled the empty space where Mahni sifted forward through the memory.

"You insolent, dribbling brat!" Mother yelled at me. "Quit that crying!"

"My Queen, I witnessed it with my own eyes! I swear it!" prattled the soldier that flew my father's corpse and I to the royal

tent.

"It's Hellebore law that if one witnesses rebellion to the Hellebore crown, the witness will be allowed to execute the offender under witness of the king or queen."

Mother purred, "So eager to slay the prince, aren't you?"

"N-no, milady—My Queen, that's not it at all!" The soldier wrung his hands together. "I was just merely saying, that is all!"

Mother huffed, and everything after that unraveled in slow motion.

I could hear the soldier's dry lips smack together as he tried to form the right words.

"Rebellion is a high criminal offense," Mother stated casually, prowling toward the soldier in front of her. Her hand shot out, and a minuscule black fleck soared through the air toward the soldier. "A criminal offense, indeed."

Before the man could utter another word, he fell to the floor with a hard thump.

"What did you do?" I questioned; my voice raw from tears. I stared at the limp body in front of me, a small thistle nuzzled between his eyes.

"Punished him for rebelling against the crown, in light of pursuing the slaying of the prince." Her voice was so calm, it made my hair stand.

Darkness overtook once more, pulling my memories backwards in a dizzying whirlwind.

Father had just adorned his fighting leathers and furs. This war seemed unending, and it was wearing me deathly thin. Mother had come to send Father off, which was out of character considering she hadn't left our tent since entering the Myrnen territory. She, as usual, blatantly ignored me the entire time. It shouldn't have surprised me, but we were at war.

If I died, would she even care?

My entire life, it had always seemed like I was nothing more than a thorn in her side, but a small part of me still hoped she would bid me luck for today's slaughter.

During their embrace, she dropped something down the neck of his leathers, a trinket for luck? No, it looked far too small for that—

The scene paused, the memory frozen, but I was busy trying to stabilize myself as I hacked through the remaining poison in my veins. It felt like the world had vomited me out, purging me from its bowels. Having one's past read was always perplexing. I opened my eyes to find Mahni staring at the floor, sorting through what he saw in my memories, scouring through the entire frame as if it were a painting holding a secret.

"See?" I hadn't realized my eyes were wet with tears, and my voice a broken roar. My wings had released on their own accord, the outer tips of my feathers vibrating with aura and nearly brushing the ever-changing walls. My electric light surged through my veins, illuminating the bone beneath my feathers. My fingers curled inwards, galvanic claws crackling at my fingertips.

The rope fell from my wrists like a satin ribbon.

I lunged for the king, securing a fist full of loose skin at the nape of his thick neck.

White-hot bolts crackled down from the fingertips of my other hand, sparking against the floor. "No. Of course you don't. Because while war waged on, you were here. Here in this filthy hole in the desert, slinging Siren Scale. And, after the war? After I watched my father suck in his final breath, she blamed me. She pinned it on me. Sending me to another realm with the sole task of getting a human heart, just to haul it here so she can revive him."

"You really are naïve," Mahni said, bringing a paw to his face and rubbing it in clear, exhausted frustration. Though my fingertips warmed with the blood from his nape, the king seemed unbothered. "Naive, naive, naive. Do you not remember what happens when we die? Did those decades on earth dull so much? The realm takes us back. We do not get to be reborn; the winds take our corpse to the aether. Did you witness your father turn to ash? Because I didn't—not in those blubbering memories of yours. I'm surprised your head even fits up your ass with those stupid Fae ears." He loosened a mocking laugh.

Something in me fractured.

He was right.

I hadn't witnessed the true death of my Father—just his downfall. I could hardly remember what happened after he had fallen; the only memory I had was of the immediate, suffocating grief and my following banishment. Mother hadn't even held court about my supposed murder of the king...

Aura spilled from my pores in white clouds, my body encapsulated in a shroud of pulsating light. Thunder cracked through me, vibrating around the room. With one gust of my wings, I had the king turned over and pinned against the floor, my hands sliding around his thick throat as I hovered above him. The lightning from my fingertips popped as sparks flew in a rain of white-hot molten light. The stench of burned hair filled the air.

"What will you do, boy? Cook me from within? Be known in the realm as a two-timed king slayer?" A vile smirk stretched across his muzzle, and rage shrouded my eyes.

I could feel it—that insatiable urge. I could do just give in. Marry the electricity in my hands with the internal volts of his heart, turning his organs to ash.

"King Mahni, the realm's jester." I tightened my grip, feeling the shift of his esophagus. "The fake persona, lylan blood, a whole show. Just for me. And to what? To capture me and send me off to my mother in hopes of saving your own ass?" I couldn't help but release a crazed laugh.

"She's got her games, and I've got mine. Everything is a wager, princeling." he spat, then coughed. His smirk remained even under my grip. The room was a kaleidoscope of shifting scenes and colors, the king's internal qualm evident around us.

There was a subtle shift in the air. My right wing twitched, spearing straight behind me and creating a crater in the wall at my back. Warmth slicked my feathers as a wet slurp sounded from the other side of the wall behind me, followed quickly by a heavy thud. The unfortunate target's heart pulsated on the tip of my wing as I dragged it back through the crater I had created. I arched both of my wings over my head, the tips just barely reaching the ceiling, though the heart grated against the texture of the ceiling before I dropped it to the floor with a sickening thump.

The swirls of colors surrounding us settled. The ceiling, floor, walls—all of it became a sterile white. No texture, no shadows. It was as if we had been suddenly transported into a crisp white box while the heart quivered on the floor, blood leaking from the ventricles with its final pumps. Mahni's saffron eyes turned in the direction of the heart, his slit pupils turning into black saucers.

"I came here to receive a reading. A *true* reading. Which is what you will give me, or I snap this fat neck of yours. I assume we're somewhere in your estate, and I wouldn't mind seeing what color flames erupt from this cesspool you call home," I snarled.

The fur around his neck was burned through to the soft, fine top layers of his skin as the smell of hot, crisp flesh wafted around us in rancid tendrils of smoke. The room darkened as the floor began to glow. I relented my hold on him slightly.

Blue, shadowed bodies emerged from the floor, linking hands with one another as they grew in size until they towered over us. I could feel my eyes try to roll back into my skull as the sapphire shadows began sashaying around us. High- pitched whines filled the air as the figures moved with intense speed, their bodies merging into one as they zinged around in their circle.

Images began to form. A shadow of bodies appeared on what looked to be the floor. One of the shapes took on the outline of a woman, her hair falling in long waves around her bare body…A golden thread formed in the center of her sternum, unspooling like yarn as it fell from her chest like a searching tentacle. An equally bare male figure with the blackened wings of a raven materialized at her side, the tentacle of light coiling up his leg.

Searching…searching…searching. Until it slithered into the center of the man's chest. The slackened thread turned tight, bouncing at the tension. The two bodies turned toward one another. A duo of birds materialized next, a raven and the shadow of something white—

Mahni's body jerked hard under my grasp, a growl rumbling in his chest.

"Now release me," he demanded.

Impossible.

It wasn't enough. I needed to see more. But I could sense he was rallying with an aura. I couldn't waste time here. It was clear to me that I had been nothing more than a stubborn fool trying to regain the approval of a deceitful, hateful mother. It stung—and I feared it always would—but my name, my heritage, and my title be damned. I needed to stop a tyrannical queen, but now I needed to figure out what to do with Lucille, too. First though, this bounty on our heads needed to be sorted out.

For now, everything else would have to wait.

I needed to get to Lucille.

Immediately.

CHAPTER 20
LUCILLE

"I don't understand. We're underground but we're also…outside?" Sweat dripped down my chest, pooling in every nook and cranny of my body. "I mean, this place has skyscrapers, and I can see the sky—or skies? And you're telling me we're just under some dunes in the middle of a desert? How does that even make sense?"

The city was a cyber-tech neon metropolis hidden beneath the sand. The streets teemed with creatures straight out of fairytales, and it took everything in me to not gawk! My body bobbed between the frames of Cyx and Seymour as we wove through furred and scaled bodies down another alleyway. The foot traffic died down the deeper we walked into the alley, as if we had crossed an invisible border. The bustling street life and neon lights immediately cut off at the last quarter of the alleyway, where its mouth opened to a near desolate street. Beyond, it was empty except for a building that could be described as dark, dismal, and rundown. Seymour smacked his lips open to reply, only to be cut off by Cyx.

"Mahni. Illusion," Cyx grumbled as he walked ahead of us to a door that blended seamlessly with the dank stone wall. The soft version of him had disappeared in that garden, his quiet, broody self-restored and here to stay.

It was nearly impossible to discern where the stone ended and where the door began. What was most strange was a miniature doll house-sized door frame that sat right above a stone knob subtly protruding from the wall.

Cyx tapped the nail of his forefinger against the miniature door. Seconds later, a small pink body opened the door, arms wide and waving. My eyes nearly fell out of my skull upon seeing the tiny thing. I looked up at Seymour, the question of what the hell the tiny creature was written all over my face.

The little door made the smallest slam as it shut, followed by sounds of rattles and clicks. Cyx grabbed hold of the handle and pulled hard, the sound of scraping stone echoing off the walls of the alley as the edges crumbled softly. The door opened to reveal a warmly lit room that leaked a flickering orange light onto the alley way pavement. Strong scents of honey escaped, caressing my nostrils.

Seymour dipped his head and laughed quietly in my ear as he jostled my shoulder. "Nothing here will ever make sense if you don't start accepting what you're seeing for what it is."

Cyx charged in ahead of us, waving a hand for us to follow.

At least this place did *not* have naked, six-breasted *things* dancing around the room, nor did it have women dancing in cluttered cages on the ceiling. No, this spot felt more like a hole-in-the-wall bar or a speakeasy whereas the other clubs we had run through were all mostly the same.

We had developed a routine—walk or run, dash down an alley, find the door, knock, enter, run through the back door.

Repeat.

Every back door seemed to spit us out in a different part of the city. I tried to watch closely when Cyx rushed us through the back doors, trying to see if it was his portal magic that allowed us to pop up in different spots, but it didn't seem so. Each time he'd grab a door handle; he would wiggle it with a particular pattern—almost like a code.

The energy in here was significantly more tolerable and far less disgusting. It was almost comfortable. Although there was a black translucent cloth over each light structure on the ceiling, I squinted and realized the lights were actually birdcages with giant glowing bugs within, which I could barely see through the cloth.

It made my teeth itch.

It was a neat light source, but with all the supposed aura-magic that many allegedly had…This place couldn't have electricity?

I studied the sleek, watery black walls as my feet glided along the floor. Thankfully, this place was nearly empty save for someone unconscious nestled in a black, plush velvet crescent booth in the far back corner. A soft jazzy melody hummed through the air.

Every step was grueling, and my feet were screaming. I eyed the chairs longingly.

Something glimmered in the corner of my eye. A petite—more than petite, actually—pinkish figure walked along the bar top. They were no taller than six inches, if that. They carried a roll of napkins on their shoulders, dropping the comically large linens in an organized pyramid.

The pink creature appeared bare bodied except for a simple charcoal colored apron hanging over their shoulders, covering their front. Their opalescent eyes flickered to us for a moment, then they gestured for us to come in faster before getting back to work.

I liked this spot way more than the previous places we had cut through, and I felt like I could finally catch my breath. Not to mention, I didn't feel the skin crawling urge to submerge myself in boiling water to scald off the feeling of hungry, curious eyes.

I leaned into Seymour, whose arm I was still tucked under. His hand had been mindlessly stroking my hair since entering the bar, and it was oddly comforting. Something about him was different from the other two, and he almost made me feel safe. I leaned into him further, hoping he had some type of power to read my mind and let me sit. I knew if I asked him, he'd probably let me, but Cyx was on a strict mission to adhere to his prince's orders.

"Pixie," Cyx offered plainly.

Seymour kicked his leg back and closed the door behind us, then dipped his head until he was almost eye level with me. He pointed at the working pixie. "We're at the edge of the city. Pixies run these hole-in-the-wall spaces. Fewer locals, fewer wanderers. Less everything. They don't have much aura. Just enough to make their sugared mead."

I followed his finger as it moved, noticing there were several other pixies of varying shades of pink behind the bar. They darted from bottle to bottle, their tiny hands glowing faintly as they pressed them against towering crystalline jugs, illuminating the liquid within.

"Pretty useless things, honestly. Kind of cute if you don't look too closely. But they do make a damn good mead. Earns them just enough respect to avoid getting squashed like bugs." Seymour shrugged and straightened, laughing to himself.

I didn't know what he found funny. It seemed like every living thing in this hellscape of a place held meaning. Everything had a role, a purpose. Granted, some creatures here seemed like they were treated no differently than if they were material objects—I respected the social structure for the most part. It must feel nice to know you held a level of importance.

Still standing in the middle of the barren bar, I watched the pixies work. Tiny bodies ran around one another like worker bees as high-pitched chatter bubbled from their lips. Their minuscule wings were iridescent, as if they were carved from moonstone, and the blue-hued flash of their wings contrasted hypnotizingly with their blushed skin. I loved the way they moved, and they *were* kind of cute. Most things I'd seen so far ranged from questionably human to terrifyingly *not* human in any sense, but these little things were the most pleasant of them all by far. It felt almost disrespectful to take my eyes off them.

"Well, I do feel that we all deserve to drink! What do you say?" Seymour exclaimed, running his fingers down the length of my hair once more, his warm hand resting on the bare skin of my lower back.

I could feel his eyes on the top of my head. I already knew he was beaming that sinister—yet kind—Cheshire smile down at me, but I couldn't peel my eyes from the pixies.

Opal eyes. Iridescent wings that looked like stained glass. Heads with…tendrils? Feathers? I wasn't completely sure, but the way the colors melted together on top of their heads made them look like precious sentient gemstones.

From the corner of my eye, I caught Seymour reaching forward to slap Cyx on the shoulder. Cyx evaded the contact but shot a lethal look at Seymour.

"The gateway. The prince made the gateway the meeting point." Cyx's words were so clipped, I almost wondered if he'd ever felt an ounce of happiness in his entire life.

"Oh, don't be a baby, Cyx! Come on, the gateway is what? A brisk walk north? We have run through—literally run through—enough clubs, streets, alley ways," Seymour remarked. "Besides, the girl probably needs something to drink, right?" He shot me a curious look, his breath brushing against the inner shell of my ear and sending shivers down my spine.

I looked at Seymour and gave him a half smile, my cheeks warming. To my surprise, I still wasn't thirsty, and I still felt great despite all the running we had just done. Albeit strange, maybe it was something about this place that had sped up my healing. Though I had to admit, the mead did look delicious.

"Bas would be proud of our hustle! No bumps in the road or anything!" Seymour continued, guffawing.

A drink *did* sound like a nice treat, and honestly, I'd just like to sit for a few minutes. Even though I wasn't in any real pain, my feet were still uncomfortable, and sitting seemed like a *great* idea.

Cyx stared at Seymour in silence. The cold hazel pools

nestled in his skull shifted to me, as he said, "One drink."

Seymour all but screamed for joy. "Excellent! Ugh, just wait until you try those little bugs' mead. The Ethereal did at least one thing right in creating those things!"

As if he were ready to crawl out of his skin if he didn't immediately have a drink, Seymour rushed to a barstool. Once again, it was as if everything here had been made for giants. There was no way in hell I could hop up onto that thing in this damned gown. If *I* felt puny, I couldn't even imagine how these little pixies felt.

"Up you go, little human!"

Next thing I knew, Cyx's hands were under my sweaty armpits, propping me onto the stool next to Seymour.

A hiss slipped out between his lips as he sat on the stool to my right so that I was between the two of them.

"Can you at least pretend what we are doing is serious?" Cyx growled as he peered over his shoulder, rapping his knuckles against the blackened bar top.

One of the pixies buzzed over, its wings whirring at such a pace it gave the illusion of floating. I couldn't help but be enamored. The pixie fluttered up to be eye level with Cyx, twitching in the air like a hummingbird.

Cyx puckered his lips and loosed a symphony of whistles, the sounds overlapping one another in layered harmony. As I listened, I couldn't help but stare at his lips and wonder how they would feel against mine.

Nope. Not going to crush on my abductor. Nope, mm-mm.

The pixie chittered a response and zipped away, returning

to the gaggle of others behind the bar as its little hands motioned commands.

I felt Cyx's eyes on me, but I refused to meet them.

Nope.

"So, which one of you is going to tell me why you three abducted me," I asked.

Seymour choked on the air, then laughed. "That's above my pay grade. Bas will have to answer that himself."

I rolled my eyes—I figured they didn't have the intention or balls to tell me themselves. "How do you not get sick of him? He's awful. He treats everyone like they're nothing more than shit on the bottom of his shoe."

"He's not so bad—" Seymour began.

"He's our prince," Cyx stated.

"Yeah, for the fiftieth time, I *know* he's your prince. But there's no way you don't see the way he treats Seymour. Both of you, really. He undermines you both and is an asshole about *everything*."

Seymour sighed. "It's a long story, but he had a rough upbringing. He's not quite what the queen wanted him to be—he's just like the late king." He paused, tilting his head. "I don't think it helped that when I was taken into their family, the queen clung to me and took me under her wing."

"Seymour—" Cyx warned.

"I'm just saying." He shrugged.

"Say less. It is not the business of others to understand the prince, but to respect him."

I rolled my eyes again, turning my attention to the pixies.

They broke off in trios, and then the little creatures hoisted ornate glasses to us, the contents spilling over the edges. I'd made it this far, and I deserved a drink.

The mead was unlike anything I had ever tasted. Sweet, almost floral, with a hint of something verging on cloves that sent a tingling sensation throughout my body. The flavor was so densely layered that this might be the best thing I'd ever tasted.

Finally, I gave in to my impulses. For whatever reason, I craved Cyx's attention and turned toward him. He was grabbing his own pint-styled glass—how could he just act like we hadn't had a moment together back in the garden? "So, they talk in whistles?"

He glanced at me dismissively from the corner of his eye as he lifted the glass to his lips. I watched his throat move as he drained the glass of all its liquid. A loud thud sounded from beside me, making me jump. It was followed by a disturbingly sensual groan.

"Divine. Absolutely divine. You little bugs really know how to do it!" Seymour exclaimed. His cheeks had taken on a soft rosy glow, the tip of his nose pink. I slipped into a fit of giggles, my head feeling warm and fuzzy.

His eyes sparkled with delight as he looked at me. "Beautiful thing you are, Luce. That sound of yours could fuse together even the most broken of hearts."

Luce.

He reached up, brushing a golden finger across my cheek as a group of pixies returned to collect his glass.

"What's wrong, *human?* Cat got your tongue?" he purred

so low I could barely make out the words.

"Seymour," Cyx warned again.

"For someone who's not into…" I gestured to myself in the way that he had done back at the hotel. "You're a relentless flirt."

He gave me a half smile and rested an arm around my shoulders.

I allowed myself to lean into the strange Shapeshifter. He had been the kindest one to me during this entire thing, and I didn't care if it was foolish of me, but aside from that moment with Cyx, I felt comfortable with Seymour. Almost safe.

The mead had pushed away nearly all of my previous worries and thoughts, the alcohol working its way through my body coating me from the inside with thick, honeyed delight.

The abrupt chuckle from Cyx caused both of our necks to nearly break as our heads snapped toward the sound. "If it's got *at least* two eyes and a mouth, he's into it. Literally."

Seymour clicked his tongue beside me as the pixies fetched Cyx's glass. "False! Two eyes *and* a pretty face!"

That small taste of laughter was delicious. I lifted my mead to my lips, chugging the last half in sloppy gulps, then pushed the empty glass toward the edge of the bar in front of me. The liquid clung to my tonsils, warming my throat. A rush of heat spread across my body. I grabbed my hair and twisted it into a rough, messy bun, using my hand to hold it in place atop my head as the alcohol warmed me from within, making my back hot and tacky with dried sweat. I closed my mind for a moment and let the buzz hug my bones. If I tried hard enough, I could almost make myself believe I was at a regular bar with some regular guys in a regular town. It almost felt sinful to feel this calm.

"And you?" I asked Cyx. For reasons I dared not dwell on, nerves crawled into my heart as I awaited his reply.

A sharp inhale came from my right. I could feel the prickling sensation of eyes on me. My small moment of peace faded entirely, but thankfully, the buzz remained. I opened my eyes to find Cyx and Seymour staring at me, then to one another. My head whipped between the two, the fast movement making my mind whir slightly. The chittering pixies were also silent, and the only sound in the room was the faint harmony of a saxophone.

"Hair down," Seymour whispered, grabbing for the glob of hair atop my head and spreading the lengths back to their spot along my sweat-slicked back.

The sound of nails on wood sliced through the music behind me.

"Damn it," Cyx cursed under his breath. His whole body stiffened, veins bulging in his neck as he pushed off the stool, his tension evident in his rigid posture. He unsheathed one of the daggers on his arm, clutching it so tight in his fist his knuckles whitened. The sound of a barstool scraping against wood filled my ears again, one falling to the floor in a loud thud that rang through the room.

My eyes shot to the barstool, then around the room, noticing the moon shaped booth with the lone sleeping patron was empty. Someone now stood a few feet in front of the plush seating area clutching something that resembled a piece of paper.

The thing's stout frame was adorned in long black fabric,

their eyes nearly bulging out of their eerily simplistic skull as they bore into me. Their movements were beyond frantic and rushed as they suddenly dropped to all fours, the sound of palms slapping on the floor echoing around the room.

Beside me, Cyx stood in a fighting stance with his dagger raised. His other hand was balled into a fist.

"A light eater? What is a droghol doing here?" Cyx cursed under his breath as Seymour grabbed me by the arm.

"Luce, we need to go." Seymour's voice was a calm whisper in my ear, but there was an edge to it. My heart was pounding so hard, I could feel the thrum in my throat. My eyes were locked on the creature—man? —crouched on the floor like a rabid dog. His mouth was half open, a silvery string of saliva webbing its way out as I watched him slap one hand in front of the other, inching his way closer, his eyes unblinking as they scoured my body and settled atop my head.

An ear-piercing unified symphony of screeches sounded behind me. The pixies had charged forward. Tiny bodies zipped past me, spearing toward the creature. Seymour's hand fell to my lower back, his palm pressed against my skin, forcing me to move. "Luce, come on!"

"What is that thing? What's going on?" I got on my aching feet once more as the droghol gurgled, lurching forward.

"Kind of like Fae. Bad. Need to go," Seymour clipped.

The pixies had linked themselves by the arms, elbow to elbow, in front of us. Their figures pulsated with an orchestrated pattern. The droghol seemed unsure whether to look at us or the pixies, its protruding eyes shifting between us.

"Go!" Cyx urged us.

"You take her," Seymour began.

Cyx's jaw flexed. "What?"

"You take her. I can handle the droghol." Seymour shoved me behind him and reached for Cyx.

I looked between the two men.

"What sense does that make? You take the girl. Wait for my arrival. Know your place!" Cyx's words were commanding, rather than condescending like Sebastien's had been, as if they were an invitation for confrontation. Were they seriously bickering right now?

The droghol snapped its jaws as Cyx stepped toward me, mimicking Seymour's movements like a coordinated dance, each stepping around the other. Seymour caught my eye and gave me a wink as his skin began to ripple. I tried to maintain eye contact as flesh and bone turned to liquid. His pupils liquefied, reshaping as narrow slits replaced them. It took everything in me not to wince, but I held his eyes until he drowned in his clothes.

CHAPTER 21
SEYMOUR

Original above, I was so ready for this moment. My claws pressed out of the pads of my paws, the feeling of scraping against the floor sending a shiver down my spine. I had no doubt Cyx would have dealt with the droghol just fine, but I wanted it. I wanted to feel its tendons snap under my touch, and I wanted the satisfaction of doing it in my smallest form.

Lucille watched the whole transformation and didn't even look away. She was as admirable as she was beautiful. If only I could scoop her up and whisk her away—but I had other plans for her.

CHAPTER 22
LUCILLE

I couldn't take my eyes off Seymour. Would he be okay against that thing? As a little cat? Surely, he could have changed into something bigger?

The droghol threw its head back. The bottom of its jaw remained stationary as the back of its head rested on its spine and it let out a blood-curdling scream. A flash of white flew toward the creature.

It was Seymour.

It was hard to see through the pixie's harsh light, but Seymour latched onto the droghol's open throat. I caught frames of Seymour burrowing his tiny, snow-kissed snout into the monster's throat, his teeth gnawing at its flesh.

Cyx's hand found mine. His grip tight, he yanked me toward the door. He was still cursing under his breath, mumbling orders to me, but all I could hear was yowl-like cries from Seymour along with the sound of flesh ripping. My lungs felt tight with worry for him.

The smell of wet brick filled the air as we exited the tavern. Cyx's words came out stern and fast. "Do not let go of my hand. Keep your hair *down*."

"That thing—Seymour—" I began, but it felt like my lungs were being crushed. "You should be helping him! There's no way he can fight that thing on his own!"

I tugged against his grip, urging him to go back inside.

He refused to budge, making my breathing grow frantic. "He'll die! Didn't you see him? He was so small compared to that thing!"

"Stop! Stop talking!" Cyx shouted. My heart stopped at his tone. He took the opportunity to tug me in his direction, breaking out into a sprint down the alley.

My feet forced themselves to keep up with the pace, and somewhere in the back of my mind, I realized somehow, they weren't raw and bleeding.

Cyx's jaw moved like a metronome, clenching and relaxing with every other breath. His eyes were a well of emotion that made me feel uneasy.

If even this brick wall with eyes was reacting, something had to be wrong.

We crossed into a part of the city that was beyond rundown. There were no neon lights along the street, and it looked like the majority of the businesses had been boarded up.

"Faster! Pick up your feet. I need you to be *faster*!" Cyx barked down at me, but I was already going as fast as I could. Every three steps of mine were easily half of his single stride.

Looking ahead of us, I spotted two bodies huddled against the opening of another alleyway. Just as one lifted their head to look at us, the other doubled over and fell on to the ground. The first waved their arms frantically, rushing over to the fallen body. The kneeling body's head suddenly tossed to the side as if they had been hit with something, their body falling on top of the other.

"C-Cyx." My words faltered between burning breaths. I was met with silence.

We kept running, our pace turning into a full sprint. As we approached the two bodies, I spotted the hilt of a dagger protruding from the temple of one of them. Was that from Cyx? Anxiety seized my heart. This was too much. My emotions, everything I had kept bottled up, it all began to boil over. Being abducted, the verbal attacks from Sebastien, it was too overwhelming. Something in my mind snapped, short circuiting.

I couldn't do this anymore.

I stopped abruptly, feeling the skin of my soles tear as Cyx kept moving, dragging me to fall painfully to my knees. A sob ripped through me, a mix of agony from the pain and pure, suppressed emotion. I couldn't stop staring at the bodies that were pouring blood onto the pavement, their skin flaking off in ashen pieces into the air. The coppery smell was so strong I could almost taste it. My stomach convulsed, mead and bile coating my tongue.

"Move!" Cyx's shouted at me as he pulled me forward, but I remained still. Another wail erupted from me, the sound clawing its way from every corner of my soul, bringing all the pain, fear, anger, and confusion to the surface. A steady thrum grew behind my temples.

"I can't, I can't, I can't! I can't keep doing this. Being dragged around. Why did those two have to die? Why did you kill them?" Tears fell onto my lap as I sucked in a breath, watching the air carry away the remnants of the bodies. "Why did you bring me here? Why is everything here so awful? I am tired, *so* tired of being dragged around like I'm nothing!"

CHAPTER 23
CYX

Her outburst shocked me. It seemed so out of character for her. Had her facade thus far just been faux bravery? Had her initial shock of everything finally worn off? This breakdown rivaled the one back in the hotel, but that one had seemed more like raw anger than whatever this was. Regardless, it was surprising that now of all times was her breaking point.

I listened to her cries for a heartbeat, unsure what to do. Sebastien had alluded that we should kill anyone and anything that got in our way, and while those two beings likely would not have been in our way, my purpose here wasn't to assume such a thing. It was to execute my orders and execute those who crossed our path.

Another sob tore through her.

Shit.

I couldn't let her sit there and ride this out. We needed to go.

Part of me wondered if the outburst was due to leaving Seymour behind rather than her abduction—she had seemed so worried about him, and very seldom had she brought up or questioned our reasons for taking her—and that didn't sit right with me. Could she not see through him the way I could?

CHAPTER 24
LUCILLE

"Lucille, look at me!" His grip on my face turned tender, his thumbs a caress brushing away the fallen tears. Though it felt as if I were underwater, I managed to find his clouded and confused gaze.

"I don't want to be here. I don't understand why you all took me; what you want from me. Seymour and that *thing*! Is *he* even alive? Or why you murdered those two people!" I screeched.

He winced at my words, tilting my chin up. "Listen to me. Listen to me. I will explain when we reach the Gate, but we— *you*—cannot stay here. I need you to be strong for a few more moments. Please, Lucille. Please." His eyes flickered above my head, then back to mine as he continued. "We need to move."

A faint sound of scuffling steps whispered behind me. The thought of seeing another creature sent a jolt down my spine, my blood turning to ice. I tried to turn toward the sound, but Cyx's hands held my face in place.

"You will not let this break you," he commanded. "Keep your eyes forward. We're going to stand up together, okay? Run just like before. But I need you to keep your eyes forward, and I need you to keep moving. No matter what you see, what you hear. We keep moving." His eyes flickered above me again, then back to mine once more.

I didn't know how to respond other than with compliance. I felt my mind slip back into a numbed state, though the thrum behind my temples grew more intense.

I let him help me stand, ignoring the blood running down both of my shins, the fabric of my dress clinging to it. His hands squeezed the tops of my shoulders in what I assumed was an act of reassurance. But that didn't matter, because all I noticed was him reaching for another dagger as his hands left my skin.

Seven bodies. Seven.

Four with a dagger to the head, two with a dagger to the chest, one with a slit throat as we ran past.

Seven were murdered.

Seven living, breathing, beings with lives outside of this moment murdered.

His words echoed in my head; *you will not let this break you.* I repeated them silently to myself, using them as a crutch to carry on. I could do this. He was protecting me, keeping me safe.

I will not let this break me.

It was clear we were at the end of the city as the cement turned to loose gravel, then to dirt. The gateway was severely underwhelming; my mind had painted an elaborate picture of an actual grand gateway with arching iron bars, dazzling magical lights—or whatever. Something that fit the neon scape we had just sprinted through.

No, the gateway was just a door. A plain wooden door

with a plain rounded knob. The same type of door found in basic mid-tier town apartments. The sight stood out like a sore thumb because the normalcy of it was beyond eerie.

Cyx took a position with his hands resting heavily on his knees as sweat dripped from his forehead in a steady stream. He looked to be collecting himself rather than trying to catch his breath. I wonder if the killing ever bothered him.

I took in the man before me, it was a wonder he could move so fast and be so nimble—almost graceful—with his stiff stature. My hands found my hips, my lungs burning. *I* needed to catch my breath. And my buzz from before? That was definitely gone.

"Tell me," I demanded as I inhaled deeply, trying to steady my heart and calm the nerves that threatened to overwhelm me again if I gave into them.

"Tell me!" I demanded again between breaths.

Cyx wiped his forehead with the sleeve of his silken shirt, the moisture from his body staining the fabric. He straightened as he looked to me with weary eyes etched by fatigue, his lips thinning into a contemplative tight line. The tension in the air was palpable, thick and heavy like a fog had settled around us. Part of me didn't want to know the answer, but enough was enough. I'd made it this far, and I deserved this one thing.

"Come on, spit it out! You had all those words back there. And look, we've made it to the gateway." My voice trembled as I waved a hand toward the ominous door. "I've got about half of one more traumatic experience in me before my brain explodes. The least one of you could do is tell me why I'm here." I fought with every ounce of courage and pride left in me to mask my voice and fake confidence behind each word when all I wanted was to disappear into the pressure that was building behind my skull.

"Your heart," he stated as a matter of fact.

I almost laughed. "Come again?"

His feet scuffed against the ground as he walked toward me, his eyes darkening. I shrunk back instinctively.

His words came out in a rush, each one hitting me like a physical blow. "Your heart. Bas was exiled. His mother—the *queen*—banished him for the murder of his father centuries ago. The only way for him—for us—to return was if he brought her the heart of a human. There's more to it, parts that make no sense. Beings in this realm cannot be resurrected, but Bas was so broken at the time that—well, that truly does not concern you." He ran his fingers through his hair, slicking back the pieces with sweat.

"No. It actually does concern me! So, out with it. I want it all. I want to hear it all." The words poured from me like venom.

He sighed, looking at odds with himself, like he didn't want to tell me something, "Human hearts can give beings here unending power—if the queen wanted a human heart, she wants it for power. I don't think Bas saw that at the time, but like I said, he was just so distraught and—"

"And it had to be me? You had to bring *me* here?"

He was quiet for a moment. "Would you rather it be someone else?"

"Yes! Well, no—" I pressed the heels of my palms into my eyes. "I don't know!"

I didn't want to be the sacrifice! Who would? But would I

191

want someone else to take my place? Not really. None of it was fair!

I lowered my hands from my face, white spots dancing in their place. "Couldn't she just get a heart for herself if she wants one that bad?"

"We were banished, Lucille! This was her proposition for us to be granted entrance back to the realm," he growled. "Do you think we find joy in this? In the idea that we brought you here to be sacrificed?"

I shrugged, knowing what I was about to say might push him off the deep end. "Your boss probably does."

His head snapped toward me, anger flashing in his eyes. "The *prince* finds no pleasure in this! That, I can guarantee. He is doing this for not only him, but for us! Besides, only Portal Mages can jump between realms. I'm the only one capable of doing so, so—" He stopped abruptly, cursing under his breath as if he had said something he shouldn't have.

"Listen, we were waiting in that estate in your realm for anyone—which just so happened to be you. And now, finally, we have our chance. You were the one human who entered on your own accord—the perfect sacrifice." His words were monotonous, feet still pulling him toward me.

I stepped back, but he continued to slowly close the gap between us.

"You're a sacrifice, Lucille," he repeated as if I hadn't heard him the first time. Except his voice was filled with pain. He was so close to me now; I could feel the humidity from his sweat-slicked skin radiating. I didn't even know where to begin, what to think. My thoughts refused to form. "But you're different, you—"

He sighed, stopping himself.

"You truly remember nothing, do you, Lucille? That you've been here before—that we've been here before—met before." His hands found my skin, his warm fingers wrapping around the tops of my shoulders. My eyes were open, but I was unfocused as his words crawled through my mind. The weight of his hands shifted as he rotated me, his fingers brushing my hair across my back, moving over my shoulders.

"Please look at me," he said with such fragility.

CHAPTER 25
LUCILLE

None of this made sense—the sacrifice part, sure, I guess in a twisted way. But I hadn't been here before. Had I?

His fingers were like fire against my skin as he dragged his thumbs down along the curve of my shoulder blades. My mouth opened, and what I had meant to be words came out as a pitiful squeak as my skin broke out into goosebumps under his light touch.

I tried again, successful this time. "No."

"You don't find it curious that you seemingly accepted all of this in the beginning? Didn't question the nature of this realm as a whole?" He dragged his thumb upwards. "I admit, it's taken quite a bit of sifting through my own thoughts and memories—all of them like dense fog. But I assure you…"

I was amazed that my brain hadn't leaked out of my ears at this point, especially as the fabric of his shirt brushed my back.

"You see, the only beings here with marks like these are lowly Fae whose wings get carved out of their backs upon birth. But you, little dove. You're not Fae, are you?" At some point his head dropped level to mine, his breath hot on my ear. His lip brushed against my skin as he spoke with a voice so calm and tender. One finger slid up through my hair, caressing the top of my ear. "Definitely not of this realm. Isn't that right, little dove?"

"I don't know what you're talking about," I waited for my fight or flight instinct to kick in, but it didn't. I willed my legs to move, to take me a step away from this man as tension swelled in my body, but they wouldn't.

There was no panic in my heart, no unsettling terror from his words. It felt as if he were talking to me about the weather, or about how plants grow. Something far more mundane. It was as if he were speaking to a specific part of me.

"Your heart doesn't beat as human," he continued, his lips now pressed to my ear, letting me feel every word against my skin. "We both have our secrets, little dove."

Something in me reacted like a small butterfly emerging from its cocoon. Like there was some part of me that knew this. His hand unfurled from my hair, sliding down the column of my neck to my sternum, stopping over my heart. My stupid, stammering heart that everyone seemed to *need*.

"Do you know how long I have been waiting for you?" His voice quivered, cracking as if he were on the verge of tears.

What in the actual fuck did he just say?

I whipped around to face him, the peaks of my chest brushing against his rib cage.

His pupils grew like night falling over a moss-covered forest as he smiled coyly. "For a very long time, little dove."

Like curling up next to a warm hearth, this closeness thawed any remaining frozen exterior of the panic and confusion. Each of his words nestled next to the raw attraction they sparked within me.

"Little dove," Cyx purred, his breath a ghost against my

lips. It was as if nothing he had said earlier mattered—like nothing else mattered except for us in this moment. He was intoxicating.

His hands slid up my body, landing at my neck. His palms pressed softly to my throat as his thumb and forefinger cradled my face just beneath my jaw. He tilted my chin ever so slightly up. Every fiber of my being sung under his touch, like my soul had been finely tuned to a melody that belonged to him.

His lips parted, chest heaving as his eyes locked on my lips.

I couldn't take it anymore. I closed the distance between us, stretching as high as I could onto my toes. My hands grabbed at the maroon silk that covered his chest, still deliciously slicked with sweat. There was no way I could have fought the swell of emotions that crashed over me.

When had I grown so fond of him? Or had these emotions always been there?

Something about knowing that he wanted this as much as I did, made me groan with anticipation. The moment his lips met mine, it was as if my soul tore through my flesh and evaporated into stardust.

CHAPTER 26
CYX

I sensed the prince before I heard him.

I broke the kiss, though her eyes remained closed for a moment, and she looked completely at peace. The creases that formed between her brows when she was deep in thought or frustrated had all smoothed. It was impossible to know how long our lips had been intertwined, our breaths mixing with one another's in a hungry dance. It hurt me to tell her of our plans for her—to remind her—it also surprised me that she still had no recollection of the previous times I had seen her.

That *we* had seen her

CHAPTER 27
LUCILLE

"Damn it, hurry up!" A distant, aggravatingly familiar voice called, followed by the sounds of boots scuffing against pavement.

My lips felt cold where Cyx's had been. His hands dropped from me as he stepped away, leaving me cold and buzzing with emotion. I stared up at him, his face reverted to the solemn mask void of emotion. It bothered me that he could shut off all his emotions with such ease. Would it be so wrong if he did feel something for me?

The voices grew closer. It took great effort to peel my eyes from Cyx's face, but relief slammed into me as I saw the two men sprinting toward us.

Two.

Seymour had made it.

His hair was streaked with what I could only assume to be the droghol's blood. Beside him, looking satisfyingly worse for wear, was Sebastien. Sebastian was outright filthy, actually. I wouldn't have been able to fight off the smirk spreading across my face even if my life had depended on it. It looked like he'd been dragged by the teeth of a hell hound through the dankest pits of hell.

Good.

Sebastien's eyes found mine as he slowed to a stop, something in them softening. He nodded a greeting in my direction, and my wince was an involuntary reply. The two men stood next to one another beside Cyx, their chests heaving in unison. I tore my focus from Sebastien and looked at his comrade.

Seymour looked to be in okay shape, assuming the droghol was worse. I shuddered internally, knowing I shouldn't care about him. And in hindsight, he was probably showing me kindness out of pity.

"The queen has a bounty a on us," Sebastien panted, his words like an irritating gnat in my ear. "Glad to see you both made it here just fine. Are you okay hu—Lucille?"

I could feel Sebastien's putrid eyes scanning me from head to toe as if they had sprouted hands and groped at me.

Why do you care? I wanted to scream. *You dragged me all the way here to quite literally sacrifice me. Am I okay? Obviously not.*

Pissant.

Keeping my eyes on Sebastien, I walked past him and toward Seymour, who greeted me with a warm but exhausted grin. "Hey there, Luce."

Everything in me wanted to wrap my arms around him, but I held back. It didn't feel right when I didn't know if his kindness had been out of pity.

But I was defeated. Utterly defeated. I couldn't kill these guys. I couldn't run. I couldn't hide. I didn't even think I could cry anymore. I'd rather be stuck in the numbing loop of complacency rather than whatever this shitty dissociative realization had been.

A hand touched me, and a small flame ignited.

Cyx.

But, to my greatest displeasure, this one was far too cold.

"I asked if you were okay," Sebastien stated.

"Do you seriously never shut up?" I growled and snapped my head toward him. "Can't you just leave me be? I'm here. You got me. You got your sacrificial lamb."

His eyes widened, hands raising.

"What?" I continued, my voice rising in volume with each word. "Am I okay? Yes, I am okay. Yes, my *heart* is okay. That's what you really want to know, isn't it? You pointy-eared asshole."

Seymour looked between the two of us nervously, either unsure of how to diffuse the tension between me and Sebastien, or just too exhausted to try.

"What? Now you have nothing to say?" I snarled at Sebastien. "It must be amusing to pluck a random girl from her life and drag her into your twisted little ritual, isn't it?"

His hands lifted higher in the air as if he were signaling for a truce. Why wasn't he fighting me? He seemed to love flaunting his title and commands, but now he chose to be silent? Without his retorts, the entire exchange turned quickly from heated to awkward. The silence was loud.

"I was only asking." His voice trailed off. "I—I just wanted to know if you were okay."

"Only asking," I repeated incredulously. I took a step toward him, my hands balled into fists at my sides.

Did he really not care that I know his plans for me?

"You selfish, arrogant, little pissant—" I cocked back my

fist, but arms wrapped around my torso and pulled me backwards.

Seymour's arms.

"Lucille, stop," he scolded. "Just stop."

I looked up at the blood-soaked Shapeshifter holding me to his chest, and my heart betrayed me as my tension eased in his friendly embrace.

"Stop, okay? It's been a very long day for all of us," Seymour began. "But as Bas had said, the queen—the Hellebore queen—has a bounty out on us. We can't stand here and taunt each other right now." His serious tone humbled me, and suddenly I felt embarrassed for my outburst.

Sebastien nodded at Seymour's words. "We need to keep moving. Anger, realization, exhaustion, whatever it is—all of that aside, we need to figure out our next move. Mahni informed me that Mo—the Hellebore queen—has been wiping out territories since our banishment. I didn't get details on whether she's killing or taking prisoners, but if what he said was true...this complicates things significantly."

"Right, right. Cyx?" said Seymour.

Cyx's boots crunched against the pebbled dirt as he stepped up beside Seymour. My eyes shifted to Cyx's; his face still void of all emotion. Silent.

"We walk through the gateway. We'll be on the outskirts of Vihn, and Cyx will jump us to Myrnen from there," Sebastien stated.

Seymour stiffened.

CHAPTER 28
SEBASTIEN

What Mahni said—what he had shown me—if it were true, then that complicated things. Would I be able to trust his words and the reading? He had already fooled me once, but would he deign to fool me again about a matter as destructive as someone destroying other territories? It wasn't that I didn't believe my mother could do such a thing; she could, and would have loved doing so, but I wasn't so sure I could trust my instincts anymore when it came to him.

Mother had always been starved for power, even back when I was a youngling. She would argue with Father, day in and day out, about the proper way to rule Hellebore. She had been all too aware—all too eager—that our army was fiercer than that of the other territories'. But my father had been too gentle, too fair, and despite trying to prove to myself—to my mother—that I was stronger hearted than Father, I knew that I had grown to be just as soft as he had been. I couldn't wear that mask of ice anymore. It wasn't me, and it hadn't been for some time.

I knew now that the reason for our return was nothing more than for her to consume Lucille's heart to harness more power. To use that boost of aura to complete her self-driven mission to take the realm for herself. How far had she gone, and how many territories were left? Was it possible to stop her if she'd already claimed so much?

And what of Lucille? How could I protect the realm while also protecting her from the realm itself?

Suddenly, my banishment no longer worried me. The chains that had dragged me down snapped. I would have to do it—protect Lucille—if what Mahni had shown me was true. If she and I really were tied.

I would protect her, even if it meant the realm burned under my mother's reign, and I burned along with it.

CHAPTER 29
LUCILLE

"Or," Seymour said. "We portal to Brenstok. Would that not be the quickest route to Hellebore? Bas?"

There was a pause as the two men looked to the prince who appeared to be lost in a world of his own. We stared at him in silence until Sebastien blinked away his thoughts and moved toward Seymour.

"We walk through the gateway. Cyx will jump us to Myrnen," said the prince.

A flash of pain flew across Seymour's face at the mention of a place, then he pulled me tighter to him as the words fell from Sebastien's lips. The prince reached for me, grabbing me by the wrist and tugging me from Seymour's embrace.

"She walks with me."

There I was, yet again, being dragged around by a man.

I looked over my shoulder to Seymour, who moved in line behind us. Cyx had already taken lead ahead of us.

Cyx stood solemnly at the gateway, his hand already on the handle and his eyes fixated on Sebastien's, awaiting a silent command. The moment he opened the door, a musty, cold breeze leaked from the hinges, exposing a dark abyss.

I tried to pull my wrist free from Sebastien's grip, but his fingers only tightened. I didn't know what I had done in my lifetime—or any lifetime—to deserve this. To end up here with these three assholes, to be their little pawn. But one thing I did know was I did not want to walk into that! The darkness soured my stomach. Alarms in my head screamed at me to turn and run.

But I knew that wasn't possible, now or ever. That had been made clear.

But walking into *that*? It reeked of pain. I'd rather gnaw off my own arm and watch Cyx behead thousands than enter whatever the hell that door kept locked inside.

CHAPTER 30
SEBASTIEN

I couldn't stand being in the presence of the Gateways, and as I felt Lucille tug her wrist back, I wondered if she could feel the gateway's aura, too. I wished she knew she was safest with me. Just me.

I slid my thumb along the top of her wrist, feeling her tense. My heart winced, knowing that the reaction was from distaste rather than from excitement. Her gown, though filthy, shimmered as I pulled her in front of me, sending a cascade of light across the darkness of my shirt as she wordlessly obeyed.

I gently turned her so she was facing me. If only she knew that if she asked me to take her away from all of this—I just might. I took in that beautiful porcelain face. With a sigh, I pulled her into my chest, wrapping my arms around her tiny frame. She tensed again, but didn't fight it, allowing me to pull her in closer. I could pawn her off onto my comrades, but I'd be damned if I let them touch her anymore.

I dipped my chin, my lips brushing against the top of her head.

"I need you to hold onto me. Gateways are notoriously fragile and can easily become aggravated. They're—I don't know how it will affect you, but focus on your senses. What you can feel, smell, hear…It will keep you connected to yourself." The soft strands tickled my lips as I felt myself giving in.

My cold exterior was breaking down, icy brick by icy brick.

I refused to be the prince, the man Mother wanted me to be.

She cautiously slid her arms around my lower torso, her hands interlocking behind my back. Not quite an embrace, but it felt all the same to me. I moved one hand to the back of her head, intertwining my fingers with the strands of those dark waves, my other hand wrapping around her waist as I lifted her. As if by instinct, her legs curled around my frame.

Original above, if I knew a place for us to hide away from all of this, we'd be in the air in a heartbeat. I pressed her head to my chest—my heart—hoping that she would hear all the things that I dared not say.

I looked to Cyx, who stared at us with lethal eyes. A warrior ready for whatever was to come. I didn't need to look at Seymour to know that he was watching me. I could feel his wormy aura prodding my mind, wondering why I was still closed off to him.

"Seymour, you're first" I nodded toward the door. He passed me, scowling. Such a pest. Without so much as a remark, he disappeared into the thick black abyss, the substance wobbling as it consumed his body. Cyx moved, positioning himself behind Lucille and me.

"Remember what I said," I whispered to her. Cupping Lucille's thigh in one hand, my nostrils filled with the remnants of the elixirs she had used in the hotel. I could devour her whole, and that still wouldn't be enough.

I waited a few breaths after Seymour disappeared into the darkness before I edged closer. The walks through the gateways were always brief, though it was better to be safe rather than sorry. That, and the first step was always the worst, so taking it one step at a time ensured the ability to defend oneself.

It was a risk to go in with Lucille because going in pairs meant we could meld minds with whomever we entered with, due to the gateway's aura allowing us to see every portion of someone's soul—stripping us bare. But I thought it more foolish to send her in alone. There was no way of knowing what it would do to her brain, and I didn't think a human had ever gone into a gateway before.

Whatever happened would happen. I needed to keep moving forward.

I did have to admit there was a sickly, selfish part of me that was eager to look into her soul. To see the stars from which her body had formed, to bare my soul to her, to show her I wasn't a vile being. That it was a mere mask. To show her what Mahni had shown me.

The gold thread that tied us to one another.

Obsidian enveloped us. I felt her tense as the substance encasing us shifted into shapes.

Yes, my soul whimpered.

My body dissolved into a weightless essence of self, and I opened my mind fully to her mind, opened my soul fully to her soul.

CHAPTER 31
LUCILLE

I could feel his breath, and I used it as a metronome to keep me grounded. I didn't love that he was the one bringing me through the gateway, nor did I like his sudden protectiveness of me, but I couldn't imagine going through this alone.

The air was heavy with emotion. Longing, curiosity, anger, pain, and resentment. So much resentment.

Images formed in the darkness, and his voice filled my mind.

This war had lasted months. What began as a scouting mission had evolved into an all-out war for territory. None of it made sense. In the first weeks, scouts had been sent out to commune with the King of Mrynen to form new trade bargains. The poison of our family flower for Shifters to join our armies.

The details were never fully given to me, so I didn't quite understand how it had developed into this war. So, so many Shifters had fallen. The pink flowered trees covering their land were now stained scarlet as furred bodies of every form lay mutilated, their ashen flesh filling the air as bodies decomposed to soot.

There's no way my father had condoned this war. His kinship with the neighboring territories ran heavy and deep—how had things gotten so out of hand?

The scene changed, my heart clenching at the sight of all that death. These were his memories, I was sure—

My hands were warm. Sticky with blood.

There was not a single part of me that wasn't aching, bruised, or lacerated. I struggled to make sense of my surroundings, the air heavy with smoke and the sounds of death. My skull pounded; my brain ached so fiercely; it was a challenge to see straight. I could feel wetness slipping out of my ear canal, down my neck. I'd been pushing myself far past my limits. Forcing aura from the land to fuel me in this battle, and it was wreaking havoc on my brain—I'd been utterly depleted of my own reservoir for days...weeks. No Fae, not even royalty, could abuse their aura for so long without reaping the mortifying consequences.

I had scorched thousands. Women, children, their elders—scorching them from within. Turning their organs to ash.

I closed my eyes. I didn't want to see anymore, *hear* anymore. His pain was so immense, as if it were my own. The pressure behind my temples flared—

My father was dead.

"What is going on? Wh-what happened?" The manhood in my voice had fractured wholly, a broken child shining through.

"Silence yourself, Sebastien! You are no longer a prince of mine. I saw what you did, king slayer!"

"No." My throat ached with the word, my mouth filling with invisible flame as my mouth sealed shut. I tried to rally aura from the blood-soaked land beneath me, but the effort was fruitless as warmth oozed from my ear.

My mouth watered as nausea took me. I wanted all this to stop. I tried to speak to Sebastien, but another onslaught from his memory washed over me—

I braced myself for the heartbroken wail of my mother to fill the space, but her silence hung thick in the air. She didn't even bother to look at my father's body lying at her feet, her eyes fixated only on me. Her face twisted with sickening delight.

"Queen Callahan," a voice said from behind me.

CHAPTER 32
SEBASTIEN

I was at a loss for words as the darkness erupted into brackish waves crashing on top of me. My spirit flinched, cowering in anticipation of the downpour of salt water. My nostrils filled with the sweet scent of flowers.

Lucille.

My fingers twitched, feeling foreign but enjoying the smoothness of her skin. It anchored me. Her heart—that precious heart—pounded through her flesh and bone against mine. I tilted my head down to hers and pressed a small kiss to the top of her head as an apology—and invitation—to see all that made me who I was.

Movement caught my eye, and my pulse quickened with eagerness. The air shifted as a small, oblong ball of white formed. The image sharpened with each of our steps, the lines of the shape solidifying. A thrum developed in my ears that worked its way deeper and up into my skull. I couldn't make sense of what I was seeing. Going through this gateway with her should have shown me the entirety of her being, her mind, her emotions.

But this?

It was eerily barren, as if she were made of nothing.

A slow, soft golden light emitted from my chest. I breathed a sigh of relief.

Finally.

The whimper of light started faintly, like a candle on the precipice of being extinguished. My skin warmed as the light grew more stable and bloomed from my center—no, from Lucille. I peered down.

Our tie.

The light moved, soaking through her and shooting out her back. It grew, morphing into something that resembled a tentacle before spearing for the oblong shape. Curiosity rivaled my disappointment. Had Mahni lied about the tie?

Had I trusted his reading too blindly?

If the reading were false, did this mean my fondness of her was nothing more than my own developed adoration? While I was fine with the realization, the idea of a soul tie with her was—well, I needed a love like that.

I watched as the beam made contact with the shape. I couldn't make sense of this, but I continued on, one foot after another. The cord of light shortened as we neared the—egg?

What was this?

The light flickered with each step now. As we approached the shape, I could see it wasn't an egg, but a vessel. The vessel drank in the light permeating from Lucille's back, the fine seam along its side glowing. Pressure built behind my temples, my skull feeling like it was about to burst.

As if flipping a switch, a crack cascaded around us. Her head snapped up, nearly colliding with my chin. Her eyes were wide open and searching.

CHAPTER 33
LUCILLE

Emerald eyes peered into mine without distaste or malice. My heart pounded in my chest, matching the frantic beat of his own.

I could feel him.

I could hear his thoughts, see through his eyes as if they were my own.

It was bizarre to see myself through someone else. In me, he saw beauty. Power. Bravery.

"Tie or not, I'd make her mine. I'd show her that I wasn't the things she thought me to be." His thoughts echoed in my mind.

I watched the last few centuries of this man's life unfold in mere seconds. It was all dreadfully sad. Watching him struggle through heartache and blatant deceit, knowing it all led to this moment—his yearning to be loved and accepted by a mother who saw nothing but a failure and a pawn. My heart clenched at the realization of his deep-seated delusion and denial. His life had been ripped out from beneath him during that war. His mother had wrung him dry. He had put on such a strong front of arrogance and confidence, but it was all a facade.

This had never been about correcting his banishment, but about proving to his mother that he had worth—that he was worth the Hellebore name. Worth his title. Worth being her son. It pained me to realize that I had hurt for him so deeply, and he would never know it because the barriers around my soul were tightly woven and impenetrable.

I unlaced my hands from behind his back, resting my palm against his cheek. He leaned into my touch, silver lining his bottom lashes. There was so much suffering within him, and his soul was so fragile.

Blatantly painted all over the walls of his heart was his firm belief that I was his mate—that we had a soul tie.

But my beings couldn't form such ties to those of this realm.

I lowered my hand from his cheek, pulling him close to me. His footsteps faltered, and I could feel his shock. I held him as tightly as I could, as if the embrace itself could piece him back together.

CHAPTER 34
SEBASTIEN

It took everything in me to keep my tears from falling. To be held like this—by her. I pressed my cheek to the top of her head as I walked. Seconds felt like hours in gateways, and though I knew we were nearing the exit, not a single part of me wanted to let her go. Not now knowing that she'd seen every crevice of my soul.

Was there a chance that through all my verbal attacks and my poor treatment of her, she felt the same way?

The chance was slim, but nothing was impossible.

CHAPTER 35
LUCILLE

For once, the fog idly clouding my thoughts cleared along with the pounding in my skull.

Cyx was right. I didn't know how he had remembered it all, but he was right.

I had been here before. Not just once, but several times.

Each time, similar events ensued. None of that mattered now though, because this time, I'd found exactly what I had been sent here for.

I sighed into Sebastien's chest; it was a nice feeling. Having my mind sorted out, my memories and purpose back. I listened to his broken heart, the heart *he* yearned for me to hear. I wished so badly that I could quell all of his pain. I didn't understand how someone like him could possibly even think he could become a king, though I supposed birthright was birthright here. My pity for him felt endless. He didn't want this life, his title. None of it.

His mind was so easily swayed and manipulated. Mahni had presented him with some vague vision, a mere thread that seemed to connect our souls. The Amisaan king, known—*praised*—for his skill of illusion… and Sebastien had fallen for it.

My heart hurt for him. He was so fragile and broken, still a mere child in many ways. Every facet of his soul marred and torn, utterly riddled with grief. Desperate for acceptance of any kind. Maybe that war, along with the outpour and abuse of aura, had caused genuine damage to his brain. It had to have drilled holes in his psyche, because the naivety of that belief alone, of *his mission,* was wild.

My heart throbbed. His life had been ripped from beneath him during that war. He'd been abused, wrung dry for all that he had been worth.

CHAPTER 36
SEBASTIEN

I selfishly drew out the remainder of the walk as we held one another in silence. I couldn't even begin to muster up the words, let alone wrap my head around what I was truly feeling. I had never been in a gateway with someone else without feeling their emotions—or even seeing even a little bit of them. Something about that didn't sit right with me, but I would dwell on that another time.

She saw me, who I truly was, and that would have to be enough for now. It was more important to figure out what to do once we exited the gateway. I needed a plan soon.

I squeezed her a final time as the air grew crisper. I wished she would say something—anything. I desperately wanted to know what she was thinking, but silence remained prevalent.

Within a few steps, the dense air lightened, a sign we were close to the exit. Unfortunately, unlike the obvious entrance, there was no clear door out. Just a shift in air and density. As the darkness encasing us seemed to breathe, light slipped through the cracks of the abyss until we were suddenly enshrouded in the light of the suns.

Nothing could have prepared me for the scene we walked into.

My grip around Lucille loosened, her legs stretching for

the ground beneath her. The moment her feet touched the aggregated soil and gravel, I moved her behind me, securing her between me and the portal. The hair on my arms raised as my aura hummed.

Seymour was crouched with his back toward us, his hands shifting so that talons curled from his fingertips. I cast my aura to speak to his mind, but it was met with a mental fortress.

He'd never closed me off like this before. I could sense his alarm, but why wouldn't he let me in?

I didn't dare breathe as two grim, spindly *demons* stood in front of him. There was no reason for these things to be in this territory—Amisa bordered a sub-territory of Myrnen, a small woodland at the edge of the Amisaan desert—let alone this realm. The Ethereal could be reckless with the beings they cast away, but I had never seen a demon of this caliber in here.

I grabbed Lucille, pulling her against my back. The demons' mouths hung open as they emitted a cacophony of disturbing clicking noises. Their heads jerked erratically; hungrily following Seymour's every move as their mouths worked soundlessly.

This was *bad.*

Lucille wiggled against my grip. "What's going on?"

Morthans.

"Do not move. Keep your breath shallow," I spoke as low as I could, hoping the demons would notice only me and Seymour.

I felt her squirm again, probably trying to get a better view of our surroundings, but I pressed my back into her, willing her to still. They were too close.

If I knew there would be an answer, I'd kneel before the shrouded sky and pray that she would be spared if we had to fight these creatures. I needed Cyx, *now*.

CHAPTER 37
SEYMOUR

Sebastien had grown so used to prodding me with his aura, I knew he would try the instant he exited the gateway.

One of the morthans let out a low growl as it stepped forward, its sharp teeth bared as the other stayed idly at its side. A growl rumbled from my own throat, my bones screaming as my claws extended further.

The second morthan convulsed, its skin grisly as it sloughed off with each movement. The scent of decay carried around us in the air, and Sebastien's panic was tangible.

This was too easy.

CHAPTER 38
SEBASTIEN

I'd seen Seymour in battle, and though he was a fierce, dirty fighter, he was no match for a morthan—let alone two. I weighed the option of shoving Lucille back into the gateway, maybe even taking both of us back in there, but would it be right of me to abandon Seymour in this situation? He'd surely die, and I knew that despite whatever resentment I had developed toward him over the centuries, no part of me would be able to live with the knowledge that he had died because I was a coward.

The right morthan crouched on all fours, its knees jutting just above of its undulating sinewy back. Not much scared me, but the sight of these behemoth demons caused my mouth to dry even as they moved away from one another.

Seymour's body was taut and ready for battle, his muscles bulging beneath his jade silks in anticipation as he lowered, taking a small step toward them. He needed to strike, and he needed to do it *now*. I didn't understand the delay.

Briefly, he peered over his shoulder at us. His face had changed completely, his eyes seething, ravenously feral.

A bloodthirsty animal.

Begrudgingly, I loosened my grip on Lucille. "Stand by the door, wait for Cyx. He should be here any second. He'll protect you."

Her eyes held a particular sense of calm as she gave a small nod.

"Know that I say this with kindness, *not* as a threat. So, please…*Please* listen to me. If you run, you will die. Those demons…" I shuddered a sigh, my chest clenching and suddenly feeling sick to my stomach at the thought of one of those things getting to her. "Just stay here. Stand by the door."

She accepted my orders wordlessly as she kept her eyes locked on mine. There was no hint of fear in them. Her bravery never ceased to amaze me. Without thinking, I leaned forward and kissed her cheek.

"Don't run," I said.

Sadness swam in her vision, but she still remained silent.

A primal, guttural cry escaped from Seymour—a mix of determination and desperation. In the same moment, the morthans moved, responding with a battle cry of their own. The haunted screeches surrounded us, their tones intertwined and mind numbing. The demons' movements were fluid and coordinated. Their bodies slithering and contorting with a speed and grace that was both mesmerizing and terrifying. Their eyeless faces were a void yet seemed focused directly on me and Lucille.

Shit.

Electricity ignited my veins, my aura crackling as currents of scalding light danced along my arms, turning my shirt to ash. Pressure built between my shoulder blades, my wings begging to be released.

"Seymour!" I bellowed.

He angled his head to me, eyes bouncing from the

morthans to me to Lucille. I held his eyes when they circled back to me and nodded. The same nod I gave him several times in our history of battles together. He returned the gesture, his talons growing millimeter by millimeter.

Centuries of self-loathing—that weak, feeble, self-centered, fragile prince—tried to claw its way to the surface, but I swallowed the emotion. I refused to succumb to those thoughts, especially now.

I drew in a sharp breath, curling my shoulders inwards. The vertebrae between my shoulder blades popped as my wings burst through my flesh. The release of pressure was damn near euphoric. Lucille gasped behind me—what I would have given to see her reaction.

"Come on!" I roared, crouching. My wings extended fully, lightning crackling throughout them as sparks rained down. My eyes went to the morthans skittering around us, their jowls hanging loose as chitters slipped through their jagged teeth. I had to survive this.

"Seymour." I ran toward the one on all fours, my wings fanned out in an attempt to shield Lucille from what was about to take place. "Choose one!"

A wet screech erupted from the demon's gaping maw as it lunged toward me, closing the distance between us. I slammed my hands to the ground, my fingertips spearing the dirt. I could feel my fingernails splintering up my nail bed, but white-hot currents poured from my fingertips like a molten lava.

Using my aura to yield electricity always seemed like an arrogant display of magic, but as the light splintered into veins beneath the ground, I couldn't help but smirk.

Would this be enough?

As if my wings had a mind of their own, the black feathers shifted and compressed themselves into two thick spears that slammed into the ground. Thunder rang from them in tandem as lightning erupted through sand and rock.

CHAPTER 39
SEBASTIEN

Electric waves scorched their way up the demon's body, illuminating its crusted skin from within as grisly blood boiled from its eyeless sockets.

I jerked my wings free, propelling my body forward, freeing a dagger concealed at my thigh. In one swift motion, I threw the blade at the demon's ribs, praying it found its target and pierced the creature's vile heart.

Hissed words layered themselves in the air, forming a cacophony of unnerving sounds—I looked toward Seymour, who subtly shrugged.

The morthans' mouths didn't speak words, and the only sound emitting from their maws were unsettling clicks that hung beneath the strange hisses. It hadn't dawned on me that a demon of this status could speak through their minds until it happened.

"The queen, the queen will be pleased,"
"It's been millennia since we have seen such a delight—"
"Yes. So powerful and unending, they are."
"The queen will be pleased."
"Oh, she will, she will indeed."
"Sent for a human—"
"Returned with an angel—"

The queen—an angel?

The realization nearly winded me. *Of course*, the Hellebore queen couldn't overtake the realm on her own—even with the Hellebore army, even if she had coaxed others to join her. She had—somehow—allied with demons.

But how had she gotten her hands on morthans? I fought the urge to look at Lucille behind me. Did they assume she was an angel? I had never seen an Ethereal in the flesh, but through all the history lessons in the past, I knew they hadn't resembled something as mundane as a human, and they sure as shit didn't dwell in the Human Realm.

Vexed by the realization and the fact I had obviously failed to kill the morthan, a roar tore through me.

CHAPTER 40
SEYMOUR

Darkness overtook the sky as malevolent black clouds consumed the light of the suns. The morthan Bas had attempted to kill was dying a slow, painful death. I could smell its insides as it turned to ash.

He was never much of a fighter. Even during battle practice when we were younglings, he had always been cowardly, so this outburst of unyielding power and anger had astonished me. The Hellebore prince—the Prince of Crows—finally decided to man up.

I huffed a laugh. Since our return to Nyria, he had been so arrogantly demanding. I saw through that mask the instant we entered Ehn. It sickened me—disgusted me—to see him flaunt such faux confidence, to treat me as nothing more than filth, and to treat Lucille with such disregard. I hadn't intended on enjoying her presence as much as I had—it was truly unfortunate, unfair for the both of us, really.

I glanced at her; her face was pale, but her eyes were fearless.

My heart winced. I knew she had grown fond of me, too.

The sky opened with a deafening crack. Lightning once again struck the dying morthan, quickening the unfortunate creature's breakdown to ash. The other one had been stalking its way toward him, but it was now a burn mark upon the ground.

These demons turned out to be painfully unimpressive, and she had assured me that this would be quick and easy. But plans changed.

I shrugged to my own inner monologue and sighed.

Had I realized sooner that she was an Ethereal, I would have gone about this differently.

My skin quaked as ripples ran through my flesh.

This was going to be utterly heartbreaking.

CHAPTER 41
SEBASTIEN

The suns broke through the dark clouds, streaks of warm light leaking through the angry, gray masses. My shoulders dropped, tension releasing as my wings rested against the dirt. I had done it.

Angel or not, I needed to make sure Lucille was okay. I pivoted on my heels and spotted her, the suns caressing her skin as they washed over this small oasis at the edge of Amisa.

She had remained at the door, just as I had left her. A smile began to spread across my lips.

Good girl, I sighed to myself.

It felt like my heart gave a sigh of its own when I saw she was unharmed. I would have to have an honest talk with her about all of it—about how I treated her, about what she was, and how she had concealed it from us all. But most importantly, I needed to apologize for everything.

I didn't understand how she was here, how she had been in the Human Realm, how none of us had caught on to the endless amount of aura that was probably buzzing within her, or what we could possibly do from here, but I fully understood that I had to make things right.

That I would burn this whole realm to the ground before I let my mother touch her or her heart.

My wings scraped against the coarse rock and sand; it was uncomfortable, but I didn't care. I was so close to her.

It wasn't a surprise to me that no fear showed in her eyes. In fact, something about that actually made sense in a peculiar way.

Her mouth parted, and I smiled.

"Seymour," she whispered.

Seymour? I attempted to conceal my disappointment. I hadn't considered him during any of this, but I knew he was probably fine.

Her eyes widened, and her voice broke as it reached a deafening scream. "Seymour!"

Talons sunk into my scalp. My wings shot over my head as pain spliced through me. As blood rushed into my eyes.

"Stop!" Lucille screamed. "Sebastien!"

I curled my wings over me, cocooned by my feathers. *What the hell was going on?*

Blood burned my eyes as I tried to peer through my feathers and scan the sky. I cast my aura in an attempt to locate Seymour, but for the first time in centuries, I couldn't feel even a shadow of him.

Fear seized my heart. Sure, I held resentment toward him, but we had grown up together. Mother had forced us to become blood brothers. I would have known if he had died. I knew I would have.

Was that why Lucille had screamed his name? Had she seen something that I hadn't? There was no way.

My aura was slowly healing my wounded scalp, but the

blood still coated my eyes. I lowered my wings. I needed to find Seymour.

"Your left!" Lucille yelped.

What in the fuck was going on? Another demon?

Talons speared through my left wing as three long, curved claws raked their way through my feathers, creating a garish hole.

A scream slipped from my lungs. The pain was blinding.

My right wing sucked back into its spot behind my flesh next to my spine, but the left now hung limp as my marred feathers and blood littered the dirt.

My eyes caught a flash of white that speared above me, I tried to follow it but it moved too fast. Hurling toward my skull was a white bird. Talons with blackened tips reached for me hungrily for me, my feathers skewered at the tips.

Seymour?

I threw my hands up just in time for the talons to shoot cleanly through the flesh of my forearm, blood spraying across my face.

I flexed, sending my aura into every platelet within my arm.

Seymour screeched and tore himself from my arm, taking chunks of my muscle and tendons with him.

That shock should have been enough to stun him.

The smell of burned flesh mixed with that of the disintegrated demons and blood.

A heavy thud came from behind me, followed quickly by shuffling feet.

"What is going on?" a deep voice bellowed.

233

My vision tilted as I turned to see Cyx emerging from the door of the gateway. His longsword was already drawn.

Blood poured from my mutilated arm, my flesh hanging in loose ribbons. The pain was stifling. I was so lightheaded. I'd lost too much blood too fast.

"Wha-what took you so long?" I could taste blood in the back of my throat as my aura coincidently failed to heal my wounds.

Cyx eyes were wild with a cocktail of emotion, but he stepped forward, ready to kill.

A bird slammed into the dirt, the sounds of bones snapping coming from the small dust cloud.

Seymour emerged, standing. Without so much as a moment of hesitation, he charged at me.

"What are you doing?" I yelled.

"Bas," Cyx yelled in warning.

I grimaced. My very being ached. I couldn't make sense of this.

"Stay with Lucille," I called back to Cyx. I needed to resolve this on my own.

Seymour had chosen his baseline man form, but his teeth were carved into tusks that jutted grotesquely as saliva poured from his mouth. He dropped to all fours, his hands clawing hungrily into the dirt.

I raised my vibration, hoping to rally the aura from the land while I anticipated his next attack.

I didn't want this. I didn't want to fight him.

I dropped to one knee and willed every molecule of aura

into my fist as I plunged it into the ground. My bones immediately shattered upon impact, and my vision grayed. Not a flash of light emerged from me.

Cyx bellowed, "Seymour!"

Seymour didn't even glance at Cyx, his focus wholly on me as he flashed a horrid smile. I slammed my fist into the soil once more, feeling my shattered bones wail as my wrist splintered further. Tears lined my lashes, but I willed them not to fall.

Not here.

Not now.

I sent a silent plea to anything or anyone who might care to listen. A weak streak of lightning cracked through the dirt toward my companion.

"Seymour, please. I refuse to fight you," I panted, feeling hollow and frail. "Please, just tell me—tell me what's going on? Why are you doing this?"

Seymour didn't so much as try to avoid my attack, accepting the lightning with grace. The currents singed his hands and feet, and though a flash of pain laced his eyes, he bore it. Then he threw his hand out.

Something small hit my chest, and his eyes darkened.

"I've been waiting for this moment from the very second your mother stole me away from Myrnen. Remember, Bas? I do. It was the summer solstice before she slaughtered my entire race. She didn't take me for employment or to lay hands on the Hellebore king, or even as a companion for you." He scoffed. I couldn't tell if he was speaking to my mind or out loud for all to hear.

"I was never meant to fight alongside you and Cyx. Or

even to become friends. Do you know how fascinated your mother was with my kind? Do you know she would force me to shift into various forms for hours on end while you traipsed after fucking floor sentries and historians? I've been held so tightly under her thumb, right beneath your nose, and you, as always, were too selfish, too arrogant, to even notice."

My vision doubled as the world around me began to move in slow motion.

My heart stuttered.

Whatever hit me was burning as though it were melting through my skin in an attempt to tunnel its way to my core.

I hadn't known I was falling until my forehead smashed into the ground.

Moving my head to the side felt like a momentous task, and I could see Cyx surging toward us, his movements appearing choppy.

"N…Stay with Luc…" My words refused to form.

Seymour's face was suddenly inches from mine. "You'll only get in the way."

The ground vibrated beneath me.

Pressure built in my chest as something sharp breached my sternum. A crack echoed in my ears—but no pain followed.

We had grown up together. We had fought side by side in battles. We had run through taverns together, laughed together.

I had been a youngling, a mere child. How was I supposed to know?

He knew I had no say or choice about the Myrnen war. He knew that.

It had been my duty to fight in the war; it hadn't been a want, nor had it been for pleasure. It was expected of me, forced upon me.

"Cy…" Blood slicked my words. I fought to lift my head, but Seymour's palm beat me to it, pressing my skull into the dirt.

"Shhh, you're dying, Bas," Seymour cooed, his smile curving around his protruding tusks. "Isn't that nice?"

"Here," he said. He was suddenly standing, grabbing my mutilated wing as he turned me onto my back, so I was fully facing Lucille and Cyx. "I'll let you watch."

CHAPTER 42
SEYMOUR

I expected to feel significantly worse. Shouldn't killing someone with whom I had grown up hold more weight? Maybe I disliked him more than I had realized.

I crouched, willing my bones to break as I welcomed another shift.

Black feathers took the place of my skin, and the world around me narrowed as I took the form of an impressively large crow. I laughed to myself, a small homage to my fallen *friend*.

I took to the sky just as Cyx lunged for me, his gold-hilted sword slashing through a loose feather. Killing him was going to be difficult, as I couldn't fight him head on.

Cyx conjured a portal below me, but I couldn't risk his success. I speared toward him, folding my wings tight to my body. At the last second, I pulled my head back with dizzying speed, and I stretched fresh talons for his flesh.

He was almost fully encapsulated in his aura when my claws met their target.

I clutched—clutched so hard—and worked to pull my body back up to the sky. His weight put great strain on my claws, his writhing body making flight nearly impossible. But I needed to get him away from here if I wanted to succeed.

I pressed my talons deeper into his flesh, feeling them

slice through tendon and muscle. I didn't dare look down at where I had grabbed him—movement was the only thing on my mind as we cleared the treetops, and I began taking us back into the dunes of Amisa.

A flash of silver glinted in my periphery. The barrel of my chest warmed with my blood. This was going to be more difficult than I had thought. This distance would have to suffice.

I released Cyx, letting him fall to whatever doom might await him.

I didn't care if he'd survive.

I needed that heart.

Now.

CHAPTER 43
LUCILLE

Holy shit, holy shit.

My mouth tasted of iron as my screams had rendered my throat raw. My stomach twisted.

Seymour had ravaged Sebastien in the most gruesome way—but why?

What should I do?

My memories had been dormant for so long, I didn't know if I would be capable of mustering up my own aura, let alone fight.

Was Cyx in on Seymour's twisted plan? There was no way I could take both of them.

And the fucking morthans? It was astonishing to see such a demon in this realm. Morthans remained in the guttural pits of the southernmost tip of the Ethereal Realm. Callahan was succumbing to the Entity.

I scanned the sky but saw no signs of Seymour or Cyx as I was frozen with fear. I was stuck.

Helpless.

But Sebastien, *he* was here. He hadn't started disintegrating yet, so that was a good sign. He was still alive—for now. If I could get to him, maybe I would still have a chance to complete my mission.

The ground shook beneath my feet.

"Luce," a voice called. It sounded so close, so familiar.

The hair along my arm rose.

No.

He was no more than a foot away. I hadn't even seen him land. He left me no time to think as he cornered me.

My back pressed against the frame of the gateway.

"Seymour." My voice broke, and it was a struggle to quell the quiver in my words. "Why? Why are you doing this? Sebastien, Cyx?"

He let my questions hang in the air as he rested a blood crusted hand on the door frame above my head.

"Where is Cyx?" I asked.

He gestured toward his chest, to the gash that ran clean through his shirt and into flesh. His head hung down close to mine as if exhaustion had suddenly overtaken him. His wind torn moonlight strands shrouded his face.

His hot breath skittered across my skin. He dropped his head further until our cheeks were level and the only barrier between us was his curtain of hair. His shoulder heaved forward, rising and falling as what sounded like laughter bellowed out of him. The sound was beyond unsettling, and everything in me wanted to run. To open the gateway and plunge through the darkness as every stardust-carved atom of my being felt like they were placed on display.

The bout of laughter ceased, but I remained petrified as he shifted and faced me directly, standing so close our noses were nearly brushing at the tips.

I raised my eyes to him, but made sure he wouldn't see how raw my terror truly was.

His eyes were red rimmed and broken. Tears slicked his eyelashes.

He hadn't been laughing.

He was *sobbing*.

A wet crunch sounded, ricocheting around the walls of my skull.

Then I felt it.

I felt every millimeter.

Every second of it.

It began as a slow pierce, a small burning sensation like an accidental needle prick or paper cut.

Then it bloomed into something earth shatteringly painful.

I held back my scream, knowing now that I would die as a failure. But I refused to go out in tears.

I bit my tongue as hard as I could. Blood filled my mouth as I sent internal pleas to the Ethereal above that this body would go into shock soon.

Seymour lowered the hand that rested above my head and gripped my chin gingerly. His voice shook as he spoke. "You don't want to watch this, Luce. I—I promise."

Then it reached bone.

"Why?" was all I could choke out as blood leaked from the corner of my mouth.

The pain was intolerable now as what I assumed was a dagger slithered its way through the structure of my sternum. A *pop* sounded as the blade broke through the thick cavity and scratched, but not quite piercing, the outer wall of my heart.

Breathing was next to impossible. Tears teased the brim of my lashes as his fist pumped the blade in and out of my chest.

I tilted my chin up, willing the tears to stay.

A soft light leaked through the growing gash as blood poured down to my navel.

I should have tried. I should have at the very least attempted to harness any power I could access. Or I could have at the least run.

Shame nuzzled its way next to the wound in my chest.

"I'm sorry Luce… I—She killed them *all*. Do you know what it's like to be torn away from your family, to be kept as a test subject? Forced to befriend the son of the woman who laid waste to your entire territory. Bas was in the way. I—There was no other way." His words came out all at once, like vomit.

I watched as his face changed from irrational anger to grief and back, as if they were different masks.

"Do you know what it's like to aid in the genocide of your own kind? Of the realm?" His eyes welled with fat tears that fell in clear pearls down his cheek. He pulled back an inch, sawing at my flesh. A small whimper escaped me.

The sound caused his face to twist as if it caused him physical pain.

This poor man.

This poor creature.

This realm—were all the beings this woefully broken?

"Here." Leaving the dagger haphazardly in my chest, he swiftly reached down to retrieve something from the hem of his silk pants—the charming shade of green now darkened with blood. He held up a small, slim charcoal colored spike the size of a pinky nail.

He swallowed deeply as he resumed sawing down my sternum.

"It's a thorn imbued with Hellebore nectar. It'll—well, it'll numb you. Shut down your nervous system. I'm so sorry, I should have done this first—I'm so, so sorry."

My eyes flickered from the thorn to his face as he reached down and found my palm, pressing the thorn into my flesh.

I would never understand what he went through, but I understood why he wanted my heart. I truly did—the power it would grant him would cause this realm to crack if he were to survive the surge of aura. The power it could lend him *would* let him face off with Callahan…But he didn't know what she truly was.

I wasn't sure even she knew what she truly was. I wanted to cry for him, to let him know that I understood his reasons. That I knew, and that my soul wept for him.

"Seymour," I breathed feebly.

"I knew the second after the droghol—the bounty parchment he held—I knew you were something…more. I have no choice, Lucille. You understand, right? I don't know if you even knew what you were. There was no other way. Please understand that. The queen, her voice writhes in my brain constantly. It drives me mad. I need to rid this realm of the Hellebore line," he said, his voice breaking even as he stayed fixated on his work and tears flowed freely down his face.

The nectar worked swiftly. It coated all my senses, rendering my body numb as my tongue swelled.

"S—" I tried.

He plunged the dagger in again, forcing the blade down. Graciously, all I could feel was immense pressure instead of pain. I heard my sternum splintering as he repeated his process over and over again, hacking his way haphazardly through bone, flesh, and cartilage even as sobs wracked his body.

"Please," Seymour wailed. "Please know, I did—I do—care for you. If there was any other way around this, I—"

"It's…Okay." The words were heavy as they left my mouth.

He fell to his knees, releasing my chin at last. Despite his hand remaining motionless on the blade, he crumpled in on himself.

Without him keeping me upright, I was pinned to the gateway by the dagger. My shoulder sagged. My vision finally begun to tunnel, and I so gratefully welcomed the darkness.

Finally…

The world faded, colors desaturating, as life left me. I fought to look toward Sebastien—I could just make out the shadows of the mutilated body that still hadn't disintegrated. Relief was a whisper in my mind.

A pulse pounded in my ears as pressure formed behind my temples.

Whum-whum-whum.

Please, please let this end.

I had failed miserably, but it no longer mattered. I just

wanted this to all be over.

These mere seconds felt like hours as my eyes lazily scanned for Cyx's form. From what Seymour had said, I knew now Cyx hadn't been a part of this.

I just wanted to see him one last time.

My vision darkened.

CHAPTER 44
CYX

That bastard. That conceiving, deceitful little prick!

It took great effort to form the portal, as my aura had become a whimper of light. Those talons had dug so deep, they scratched bone. I winced as I clutched the longsword in my fist. What he had done to Sebastien—I shook my head, my hair sticking to my skin.

I refused to believe Bas was dead.

CHAPTER 45
LUCILLE

My mind pulsed as it began to replay memories from the past. The other times I had been in this realm. It was getting so hard to keep this reality straight, but I needed to hold on—I needed to focus. My mind fractured as I slipped into a memory.

An ominous silence bloomed around us as I unsheathed my blade, eyeing the morthan in front of us, its teeth gleaming with black blood from the wraiths that now laid at its gnarled, clawed feet.

We didn't stand a chance...Did we? Morthans were hell sent. They hailed from the darkness of the Ethereal Realm. Standing at over ten feet tall, they were joint-less, gaunt, spindly, and grotesque eyeless creatures. The blood that flowed through their repulsive veins was both obscure and coveted. It could be enchanted and wielded in nearly any format imaginable—poison or cure, it all depended on how the user manipulated the substance with their aura. And now, more than ever, we needed it.

My sword glinted gold in the murky sunlight as I lunged forward, striking heavily at the creature. The morthan crouched, its body contorting just out of reach.

The two black, gaping holes where its eyes should be began oozing something grisly. It swiftly reached a clawed finger

up to the socket, collecting the fluid before bringing it to its
hollowed mouth, almost as if it were signaling me to hush as it let
out an ear splintering screech.

The fluid at its fingertip ignited with thick, poisonous
green flames, shooting straight at me.

We were running out of time.

I peered over to my angel, her iridescent skin fading to a
muted, sickly gray. The gold that glittered in the veins of her soft,
dove-like wings were winking out. She was fading.

My eyes fixated on the hilt of the dagger that protruded
from her sternum. I would never be able to rid myself of the sickly
crunch her sternum had made.

The sound of my own heart breaking echoed closely
behind.

She had been everything.
She was everything.

I fought against the fog trying to overtake my mind. That
memory left me confused; it made no sense. That wasn't my
memory—was it?

"My memory," choked a deep voice. "From the first
time."

Exhausted, I couldn't even find it in me to question it
further. My eyes struggled to focus on the form that stood above
Seymour, who was still sobbing, causing the dagger to slip in and
out of place.

Everything happened so fast.

Blurred shapes moved.

Immense pressure formed in the center of my chest, followed by a wet squelch. A scream, then nothing.

I could smell the coppery fluid before I felt it warm my skin. The pressure in my chest relented, and my body quaked as I hit the soil.

I squinted at the shape beside me. I could just make out the moonlight color of Seymour's hair, the hue of his skin—and the blade with a gold hilt that ran through the back of his neck and through his throat.

Cyx's blade.

Cyx kneeled beside me, reaching for something in front of me. There was a slight tug, as if something had been pulled from me, but I couldn't quite make out what it had been. He rested it near Seymour's body.

Crouching over me, he gently rolled me onto my back, a halo of iridescent purple bobbing around him.

"Cy…S'bas?" Words were impossible.

"He'll live. The stubbornness pooled in that body of his will keep him alive for a millennium." I could feel the warmth of his hand as he cupped my face. He feigned a laugh, but the sadness in his voice was evident.

"Se…mr?"

Silence.

My soul stung despite everything.

Everything I had just witnessed, and everything he had done. I couldn't fault him for anything. He had been right; I didn't know what he had gone through, or what it was like. But I might have done the same in his position.

The strange being that was Seymour had shown me kindness at every moment of this journey. Whether it was fake or if he had been scheming the entire time, every moment of that kindness had meant more than he could ever know.

Would never know.

CHAPTER 46
LUCILLE

I didn't know I had started to cry until I felt Cyx wiping my tears with his thumb.

"It's okay, little dove, I've got you now," he whispered. The world around me slipped out of focus as sounds turned into patterned vibrations and rhythmic thrums.

"You can let go." His body shook stiffly, his voice fading in and out as if he were under water.

"Lucille," he said my name as if it were a prayer as he carefully pulled me close.

There was nothing I could do except accept this. All of it. What was left of my heart had shattered into millions of pieces.

"I promise you," his voice broke, and I could feel his hair cover my face as he pressed his forehead to mine. "I will find you again."

He pressed a tender kiss between my eyes as he whispered against my skin.

"And I will not lose you."

The words shattered me, broke me fully.

The world went black.

CHAPTER 47
LUCILLE·PRESENT

A low rhythmic hum fills the air, pulsing with a constant rhythm.

Whum-whum-whum.

"Trial four, complete. Systemic replay has been initiated. Please do not remove

"LUCILLE CERES from the pod. Systemic replay will be ready for review in sixty seconds. Please, hold," a metallic voice chimed in my head.

A rushing fills my ears, the sound smashing against my ear drums in a pounding rhythm. A searing light shines through my eyelids, filling the blackness with a mix of sparkles and shadows. My soul pulsates, throbbing and aching as countless images, emotions, and conversations move like a cyclone through my psyche. My back arches as the information categorizes in my brain, pressure building behind my eyes.

"Systemic replay complete. Information secured," the robotic voice proclaims. The pressure behind my skull dissipates with the announcement.

"Failure."

A low voice hums, followed by a long sigh breaking through the sounds flooding my ears. A cold, clammy hand touches my forehead, the frigid skin feeling like it's sizzling against mine.

I peel my eyes open, wincing at the brightness that fills the too golden room. I snap them back shut. The shapes and hues assault my eyelids as a hazy blur of colorful bodies scuttle around, holding things in their arms. The light overhead splits into a trio of fuzzy, glowing orbs. A smooth, cold hand touches my wrist.

"Her vitals are stable," a gentle but cheery voice squeaks. "Luci, it is so good to see you awake! It feels like you've been gone forever and ever and ever! I missed you! I can't wait to hear about your jou—"

The falsetto squeal is severed by a harsh shush.

"Will you pipe down, Lotte? For once? By the hands of the Original, that voice of yours is cursed and curdled," the person groans, their voice reverberating against my ear drums like a hornet.

"Failure number four. A pathetic attempt, as always. Do you even care? Forty-eight hours until the end, and yet you still can't get it right," hisses a frustrated man. "Lotte, fetch the scribe. We need to review the reconnect."

The sound of retreating footsteps echoes through my head along with a familiar reminder of my incompetence. Slowly, I force my eyes open, dreading the blinding light that greets me once again.

The room is vast and sterile. All the oblong shapes, suspended in the air in rows in front of me, are all open. All empty.

"Four attempts to reconnect. Four failures. I will say, you are the most disappointing halfling I've seen in eons," the man says under his breath.

The man standing at my side towers over me by several feet, his eyes bloodshot and heavy with disappointment. I follow his hand as he presses a finger to my forehead, sliding it up to my hairline. I feel tiny things pop and release from around my scalp.

"Seergear deactivated," chimes an overhead voice.

"C—" I try to croak, but my vocal cords protest as I choke on my words, suddenly aware that my throat feels tight. My mind wavers on the cusp of consciousness as my thoughts blink out for a moment.

He begins touching my face again, brushing around my lips as a violent, scathing pull runs through the length of my throat like a hot iron.

Something is being yanked from my mouth.

My esophagus is raw, and the back of my tongue is metallic.

"Michael! Careful! How do you expect her to speak when you're tearing breathing tubes out of her like that?" scolds a cheery feminine voice. She clicks her tongue and shoots me an apologetic look.

"Wh-what's going o-on?" The words crawl from my throat with great difficulty, leaving my throat feeling as if it's in invisible flames.

I bring my hand to my chest where a low ache hums between my breasts. It feels like I'm moving through molasses; all my joints are stiff, like they have been locked in one position for ages. I almost feel like a statue given life. I drop my hand from my chest, the meager movement enough to pull the air from my lungs and leave me panting.

The world suddenly snaps into focus, the filmy fog over my eyes clearing as if a drug has just worn off.

My mind grows sharper by the second. I'm encased in a cylindrical pod, the walls glistening with a white, metallic sheen. A soft, blue light emanates from within, highlighting the smooth curves of the pod.

My body is suspended by straps, hovering just above a cushioned surface. The door to the pod hangs open freely, displaying its glowing symbols. I know these symbols. I've seen them before in Sebastien's library.

Cyx. Where is Cyx?

My mind recalls his fading words, the feeling of his tears on my skin as my two realities overlap.

My eyes fly around the room, *déjà vu* rattling my brain.

"Don't worry, ignore him. You know how he gets. You just focus on shaking those cobwebs off that mind of yours, okay? Here, swallow this."

The girl—Lotte, I think—cuts through my thoughts with a small smile. She shoves a yellow glob into my mouth. The sweetness coats my tongue as the substance melts instantly.

"That should help your throat, alright? Should also help with the brain fog."

My eyes lock onto the girl. The all too familiar girl.

Familiarity continues to stifle my senses. Her pin-straight hair is a soft shade of lavender with silvery, iridescent streaks. Behind her, giant white wings tuck in closely to her back, the feathers glimmering from the light and sending rainbows across the room. The smile stays firmly on her lips as she watches me swallow the remnants of the honey-like glob.

Reality slowly forms, the long-estranged pieces of a puzzle finally clicking into place.

"Lotte?" I ask.

"Yes, that's correct, Luci." Her glittering eyes crinkle as her smile grows. Her small hands work to undo the straps around me.

A sudden swell of emotions washes over me, tightness forming in my chest as the words leave my mouth in a whisper. "I failed."

I had failed. In so many ways.

"I know," she whispers, sadness dancing across her berry-colored irises. "I know. You will succeed at the next Reconnect trial. You must, and I know you will. Don't worry about that now, okay?" Her head bobs in several nods, confidence coloring her eyes.

I need that heart. I need my wings. I need to be complete. This was my fourth trial, and my fourth failure. A near-catastrophic failure, and I have one final chance to succeed.

"Halfling, Lucille Ceres," Michael starts. "You have failed your fourth Reconnect. Let these words serve as a reminder that be it blessing or curse by the Original, you have been granted the opportunity of being this millennia's Reconnect Warrior, a role assigned to each millennium's gifted halfling." He sounds as though he's reading from a scripted speech, and the words feel familiar even as he says them.

"You are a being forged from the Originals' own self-splicing. A being of two realms, Ethereal and Human. Being a

257

halfling means you are the realm's savior. You are to eliminate the Originals' dark soul—known as the Entity—that has been entombed within the aura of the Magic Realm, known now in its current age as Nyria, since the creation of realms." Michael pauses to lick his lips.

"The goal of each new millenniums halfling is to reset the cycle of the dark soul by locating its reincarnated host. Obtain the creature itself or the being's heart. Consume the heart to not only commence the reset but be rewarded with the gift of becoming full Ethereal. Reset the cycle. In forty-eight hours, you will embark on the fifth attempt. This will be the final attempt in which you *cannot* fail."

Shit. That's right.

The speech flows through my mind as I finally recall. My inner narration finishes Michael's sentences in tandem with him. I've heard this for what feels like too many times. A spur of disappointment and self-doubt fills me.

"In forty-eight hours, you will re-enter the Shell where you will undergo minor hibernation as we relocate your soul into Nyria, resetting the time line so that you may repeat the trial. Is that clear, halfling?" Michael's eyes are vacant as he waits for my confirmation. "Have you any questions?"

"I understand the goal and the stakes," I reply solemnly.

Callahan is this millennium's reincarnation. With each reset, the Entity festers within its host, its tainted aura spreading eagerly throughout the Magic Realm, resulting in famine, genocide, and terror. Her—*its*—sickness is already leaking into the Human Realm, where wars are waging, stripping the realm and

258

putting it onto the brink of collapse.

My memory is what always fails me. Each time I go in for the Reset, I wake in the Human Realm with no trace of who or what I am. Each time I enter the library, endure the same minor tortures, and each time, I succumb to the faux host's "life."

The one part that doesn't sit right with me is Cyx. He remembers me, and that shouldn't be possible. It's difficult to fully recall the first few Resets without seeing the log, but I have no recollection of him remembering me in the past. What I do know is that each time, I start to fall for him.

"It looks like you have consistent malfunctions with your memory when you reconfigure into the Human Realm. You subsequently forget your true nature, and your brain overrides the program from the Seergear and thinks it's fully human. It's baffling that the Magic Realm folk are so ignorant to your true makeup. Better for us, I suppose. Means we're doing something right. But the other side of the coin says otherwise. That means the Entity has surpassed what the Original has assumed." Michael sighs, his words flat and unpromising. "An elder will need to examine the main program. Lotte?"

Lotte nods and rushes off, leaving me alone with Michael.

"And Cyx?" I blurt out.

Michael eyes me curiously. He swipes his finger through the air. An opaque screen appears, and his eyes began scanning.

"We have no recording of any beings or creatures that hold the name of Cyx." He lowers his hand and the screen vanishes. "We watch you in real time, as with all of the other times."

"He—" I pause, unsure if I want to say what I'm about to tell him. "He remembered me."

Michael stiffens.

"Did he give you a family name?" His voice is sharp with demand.

"Andromedi," I whisper.

Michael's hands land on my shoulders, pinning me to the shell. "Did he have aura?"

I try to edge away from his grasp as a pit forms in my stomach. "He was—is—a Portal Mage."

He blanches. "And you're certain?"

"Yes? That's how we got around, mostly." I want to ask why this is so confusing.

Lotte's voice flutters through the air behind me.

"Tell me what's going on," I demand as he straightens and steps away from me.

"Portal Mages no longer exist. Those beings were closest in relation to the Ethereal," he says, muttering an incoherent curse beneath his breath. His words are rushed and breathless as he continues.

"The Andromedi were prophets. The Original—it's none of your concern. Just know they no longer exist."

"Michael?" Lotte calls, her voice closer.

"Do not speak of this to anyone," he spits under his breath. I stand in silence, nodding.

I won't speak of this to anyone, but he didn't say not to speak of this to any*thing.*

The energy in the room shifts as his eyes rise above my

head.

"Out of the shell," a hollow voice says above me. My stomach plummets to my feet as I comply and fumble from the pod, nearly falling to the floor. My legs are numb from lack of use.

I force my chin up out of respect. I hate the elders. They terrify me.

My eyes meet the many eyes of the elder in front of me. Similar to the morthans, the elders sport tall and thin frames, but they're pure white and clad in white silk. I bite my cheek, trying to remain still and calm.

The elder's movements are slow and fluid, unlike the convulsions of the morthans. I watch as it draws a slim, multi-jointed finger above the shell I stumbled from. It's hard not to stare as its spider-like eyes move in several directions, sorting through the code that appears in the air.

Seconds feel like hours in the elder's presence, but at least I can tell Michael and Lotte feel the same way by their equally rigid stance and loud silence.

With another swipe of its finger, the code winks out. I shift my eyes from the elder, knowing it probably saw me watching it. I scold myself internally. Hopefully, it'll be leaving now.

The elder is still for a moment, its team of beaded eyes clicking into place and locating their focal point.

Shit, is it looking at me?

The elder glides toward me, slowly bending at its strange hips until its torso is parallel with the floor. Its head remains straight forward, looking right at me until it's inches from my face.

261

At this distance, I can see each iris has three overlapping pupils.

I stop breathing entirely.

My mouth dries, my lungs aching for air, but I dare not breathe.

"How odd," the elder states, its mouth unmoving.

EPILOGUE
CYX

I had never known such pain could exist as I raised my head from Lucille's cooling forehead. Seymour was just inches away, his body half gone and stolen by the wind.

Her skin began disintegrating in flakes as well, fluttering in the air. Not the black sooty flakes that I had grown numb to seeing in Nyria, but in white, iridescent puffs like dandelion seeds in the wind.

"Cyx," a weak voice called from behind.

Sebastien. The prince.

I turned with hesitation—not wanting to leave Lucille's side—to find Sebastien sitting up, his eyes scanning the scene before him.

"Cyx, wh—" he began.

No words could explain what had just taken place.

I stood slowly, exposing Lucille's body as the breeze carried away the pieces of her, mixing her ashes with Seymour's. The prince shattered at the sight.

My throat felt tight. I couldn't allow myself to cry in front of him, and there was no time to console him, so I chose my words carefully.

"I haven't been honest with you."

Sedona Jessie

To Be Continued…

in book two of The Heart Chronicles.

ACKNOWLEDGMENT

I'd like to give the biggest thank you to my sweet friends who stood in my corner throughout this entire process.

Catie, Drew, J.A., Aubrey Winters, Shelby, Yesenia, and Kim; without your words of encouragement, and faith in me to pull this off, I'm unsure if I would have ever had the courage to complete this project.

A special thank you to my uncle Kyle who ever since I was little has inspired and encouraged me to dive deep into the realms of fantasy and all it encompasses.

I love you all.

www.ingramcontent.com/pod-product-compliance
Lightning Source LLC
Chambersburg PA
CBHW020128120726
47903CB00007B/2156